The Countess
and Me

Paul Knopp

June 24, 2002

The Countess and Me

by Paul Kropp

Fitzhenry & Whiteside

The Countess and Me
Copyright © 2002 by Paul Kropp

Published in Canada by Fitzhenry & Whiteside, 195 Allstate Parkway, Markham,
Ontario L3R 4T8

Published in the United States by Fitzhenry & Whiteside, 121 Harvard Avenue,
Suite 2, Allston, Massachusetts 02134

10 9 8 7 6 5 4 3 2 1

Fitzhenry & Whiteside acknowledges with thanks the Canada Council for the Arts,
the Government of Canada through its Book Publishing Industry Development
Program, and the Ontario Arts Council for their support in our publishing program.

National Library of Canada Cataloguing in Publication Data

Kropp, Paul, 1948-
    The countess and me
ISBN 1-55041-680-4 (bound).—ISBN 1-55041-689-8 (pbk.)
    I. Title.
PS8571.R772C68 2002   jC813'.54   C2002-900327-X
PZ7.K76C68 2002

U.S. Cataloging-in-Publication Data
(Library of Congress Standards)

Kropp, Paul.
  The Countess and MeI / by Paul Kropp. — 1st ed.
[172] p. : cm.
Summary: When he first meets Countess von Loewen, Jordan finds himself
obliging her by burying a quartz skull she claims is cursed. She's not your typical
neighbor, but soon she employs him as her gardener and believes in him as
nobody ever has. Jordan must now confront his own self-worth and value.

ISBN 1-55041-680-4
ISBN 1-55041-689-8 (pbk)
1. Friendship — Fiction. 2. Trust — Fiction. I. Title.
  [F]   21   2002   AC   CIP

Front Cover by Kirsti Anne Wakelin
Book Design by Darrell McCalla

To Lori,
who got me back on track.

CHAPTER ONE

The Skull

"JORDAN'S GOING OUT AGAIN," my little sister announced in her best tattle-tale voice. She was supposed to be doing her homework so I don't know why she even noticed.

My mother looked up from her little laptop computer. "Where do you think you're going?"

"Out," I said. Dumb answer, I knew, but at least I said something. Lately I hadn't been saying much of anything to anybody.

"Out where?"

"Just out." Why did I always have to explain everything? I mean, it wasn't like I was about to wander away or get kidnapped.

"Jordie's going out to smoke," my little sister piped up.

I blushed. The little rat was right, of course, but she didn't have to volunteer the truth like that. "Shut up, Miss P., just shut up."

"Jordan, we don't use that language around here," my mother said, not really paying attention to either of us. "And don't call your sister names."

I was not calling my sister a name, just a nickname. Miss P., which is better than her awful real name of Priscilla, is a short form of Miss Perfect, which she pretends to be. Miss P. with the perfect manners and the perfect attitude and the perfect report card; except I know she's tried out Mom's lipstick and hides rap CDs in her dresser. Of course, it's easier to pretend to be perfect when you're eight than when you're thirteen. Eight is when everything you do is cute and everything you want just falls into your lap. Thirteen is when most of what you do is stupid and everything you might want seems somewhere just out of reach.

You can guess how old I am, can't you?

"Don't be long," my mother concluded, waving me away. "You still have homework. You're going to end up in summer school unless you buckle down."

"Yeah, yeah," I mumbled, heading out the door.

"And don't get in troub—." That was the last thing I heard as the sound of our closing door cut the "trouble" in half.

As if anybody could get in trouble here. We live in a subdivision that is forty square blocks of nothing, surrounded by several hundred square blocks of not much, all of it located about ten minutes from downtown nowhere. It would be easier to get hit by a meteorite than get in trouble here.

But moms are like that. They worry too much. And they remember stuff, like the couple of times you really did get in trouble, or broke something, or made a total mess of something. My mom is always reminding me that once, when I was little, I tied a towel around my neck and jumped out of our second floor window onto a lawn chair cushion. Apparently I thought I was a superhero, but I ended up with a broken ankle.

So much for my early heroism.

Of course, that was back when I was little and still felt kind of heroic. After we moved out here, I started feeling mostly lonely, or stupid, or miserable. Three more good reasons to smoke, it seemed to me.

Yeah, yeah, I apologize already because it's a stupid, disgusting and life-threatening habit. And I know I smoked because I thought it made me look cool, but really it made me look pathetic. And all that. But this was my last cigarette — and they're not cheap when you have to buy them from a kid who's a crook but looks old enough to get them at a store, while I look like I'm about ten.

So I puffed away, trying to enjoy the smoke but still feeling pretty lousy. Ever since we moved to Surrey, school's been awful and life's been about as exciting as watching the Weather Channel — no, worse, it's like Weather Channel reruns. It didn't used to be like that. Back in Winnipeg I used to have friends, and do stuff. We'd all run around and pretend we were superheros, and zap the villains with our imaginary laser guns, and just goof around the way guys do. You know what it's like when you're little: you think you'll grow up and do something wonderful or exciting. You'll grab somebody before they jump off a bridge, or rush to take the bullet that's zooming toward your girlfriend, or protect somebody against a bunch of dope dealers who are beating him up. I'd do it, too, if I had a chance. The only problem out here is that I might just die of boredom before I get the opportunity.

Anyway, I finished my smoke and started walking back along the sidewalk toward my house.

That's when I saw this funny old lady out in her front yard.

I probably wouldn't have paid much attention even though it was kind of strange for somebody to be digging in a flower bed in the dark. But the thing that caught my eye was her hat. It was a weird hat — kind of red and tilted sideways, with a flower sticking up on top and some feathers going off in various directions. I mean, it would have been a weird hat in church on a Sunday morning. But on top of an old lady's head as she's digging in the garden working by the light of a flashlight, well, that's *really* weird.

The old lady looked up at me as I passed. "Well, you can stare or you can help," she said. The words had a kind of accent to them, like the w's were v's and the o's came out kind of long.

"Sorry, I didn't mean — " I began.

"Of course you didn't mean, nobody means. But I need some help, yah?"

"Help?"

"Digging. Is rock here, someplace, under this shovel. It's too much for an old lady like me, yah?"

"Yah," I repeated, stupidly, "I mean, yeah. So, like, you want me to dig the rock out, like now, in the dark?"

"I need a hole to bury something, right here, and there is no time to waste. No time. The flashlight is enough, yah?" She looked at me with this strange grin, so right away I thought she was kind of loony. Or eccentric — that's the name for a loony with style or class, but still a little gone in the head. Here she was wearing a hat, a black dress, and what looked like pearls, out digging in the garden at eight o'clock at night. Loony or what?

But still she was an old lady, and she obviously couldn't do the job herself, so I dug. The topsoil had to be pretty new, since the whole subdivision was only a year old, so it was easy to get that out of the way. But the big rock underneath was stuck pretty hard into something.

"Lady, this thing's not going to move," I said. I'd worked up a little bit of a sweat trying to get at it.

"Yah, yah, anything can move if you try hard enough. Anything." The "anything" came out sounding like *anyssing*.

"Look, I might break your shovel."

"Is only a shovel. You can do it, boy. Just use your weight — is leverage, all leverage."

"Yeah, right," I said, putting the point of the shovel in at a couple of places, then leaning on the handle. Finally I got the rock to jiggle a little.

"It's coming."

I grunted and pushed on the handle, then moved the shovel and did it again. Finally the rock rolled free. It was huge, and must have weighed as much as I do.

"Oh, good, good, good," the old lady said, clapping her hands. This made the flower on her hat teeter precariously, but the thing didn't fall off. "You are so strong," she said. "Now you roll the rock down over to the side before we put it back."

"Put it back?" I repeated. Now I knew she was loony. I'd just dug up a huge rock and now she was going to put it back where it came from. Riiight.

The old lady went into her house and came back out with gloves on her hands and carrying a burlap sack. "Now we bury this and is finished. We are safe."

Now I was getting a little spooked. The burlap sack was the kind you'd see in horror movies to carry body parts, and it was just big enough to hold a human head. In fact, the shape of the sack even looked like a head.

"Uh, now just, uh, what are we burying?" I asked, backing up a step or two. The old lady looked harmless enough, but you never knew.

"Is a skull," she said, matter-of-factly. She must have seen something in my face, so she went on, "Not a real skull, but quartz."

"Quartz?" I was feeling really stupid now, just repeating everything the old lady said.

"Like glass, only a mineral. Here, you see it," she said.

The old lady set the burlap sack down on the ground and untied the drawstring. The cloth fell down and revealed the most amazing thing — a transparent skull. It was almost the size of a person's head, shaped like a real skull, but perfectly clear. Somebody had carved indentations for eyes and fashioned an opening where a nose would have been. But the scariest part was the teeth, which were smiling in a really gruesome way.

I don't know how long I just stared at the skull, watching the light bounce around inside it, examining the dark eye sockets, amazed that something could be so beautiful and so horrible all at once.

"No, don't touch it," the old lady shouted.

I looked up at her, then noticed that I was reaching out with one hand to touch the thing.

"You mustn't touch," she said, spitting out the words. "Is dangerous even to look." She pulled the canvas back up and retied the string at the top.

For a second I didn't know what to say. My mouth felt so dry I didn't think I could speak, like I was still in some kind of trance. "I … we … "

"We must bury it. Now. *Mach schnell*," the old lady said. With that, she picked up the skull in its canvas bag and threw it into the hole. "The stone … the stone must go on top."

"But it might crush the skull," I said.

"No, the skull will survive. But the curse, maybe we will bury."

This was crazy — a skull you can't touch, a curse, a hole in the ground — but it was weird and spooky too. Suddenly I just wanted to get away from this and back to my house. So I took the shovel and used it to roll the stone back into the hole. It fell with a clunk, but I heard nothing shatter. The skull, as the old lady said, had survived.

"Now the dirt. We do neat job so no one will know where it is."

I began shoveling the dirt back into the hole, feeling like a gravedigger after putting a coffin to rest. The old lady got a rake and began using it to get little clumps of dirt off the grass until, at the end, nothing remained but a little mound of earth for a flower garden.

"Is good. Is finished."

A gust of wind came up and made the sweat on my forehead feel cold. I wiped the sweat, then found that my hands were dirty. I must have left a swipe of dirt up there, because the old lady saw it.

"Oh, I have made you dirty, and is no good. You come inside and wash up, yah?"

"Nah, that's fine," I told her. I mean, I'd helped her with the rock, but there was no way I was going into this old lady's house. There's loony and then there's crazy … and she might be one of the dangerous ones. "I'll clean up when I get home. My house is just over there."

She followed my wave and nodded. "Yah, yah, I understand. Here, then, you take this, you work so hard."

She dropped a coin in my hand. In the dark, I couldn't see what was it was. I figured she'd given me a quarter, because old people like my grandma think that's big money. Anyway, I put the coin in my pocket and said goodbye. "Thanks a lot," I said, backing away.

"You're a good boy. So good," she said. It made me feel like I was about five years old.

So I went on my way down the street while the old lady got out a broom and began sweeping her front walk. She was humming some kind of strange song, but seemed happy enough. I was just glad to get away from her and all the craziness. For maybe the first time since we moved, my house started to look pretty good — at least until I got in the door.

"What happened to you?" my mother asked, staring at me.

"I was meeting the neighbors."

"Well, you're just filthy, Jordie. Now get cleaned up and onto that homework."

"Yeah, well, I had a good reason," I mumbled. "I was — "

"No more excuses," she said, "just do it."

She didn't even try to listen. That's one of the things about her since we moved, she stopped listening. My mom didn't even wait for an explanation, just slammed into me. Lately everything I do is wrong, from not jumping out of bed in the morning to not flossing at night. Maybe it's being a teenager that changes parents, but now mom seems to treat me like I can't get anything right. And maybe I can't right now, but some day I will. Some day.

So, yeah, I did my math homework — at least some of it. And then I got on ICQ with a couple of my old friends, and then I got ready for bed because I was really beat. It wasn't until I went to throw my pants in the hamper that I remembered the coin from the old lady. I fished around inside my pocket and put the coin on my bed. In the light, I could see that it wasn't a quarter. It was something else — a dollar, an 1886 U.S. silver dollar.

CHAPTER TWO

Detention

NOW THAT I DON'T GO TO IT ANY MORE, I can admit that my old school was pretty decent. Of course, when I was there I never figured I'd really miss the place. But it was better back there. A couple of my old teachers thought I had at least half a brain, and at least I had some friends. There was Marty Mankowitz, the hustler who always had candies or smokes or something; and Huge Hugo who would threaten to sit on anybody who gave you a hard time; and Reena, a girl who sort of liked me, sometimes, a little. And Jake and Alex, my good buddies, who still emailed me, though not as much as they used to.

But then my mom got this new job out west, so I end up in this place — Alex Colville Junior High. The teachers seem to have some kind of permanent grievance against the school board, like they haven't had a new contract in twenty years and are still working summers at the Dairy Queen to pay the rent. The principal looks like the boss in Dilbert cartoons, with two little bits of hair sticking up from a pointy bald head.

And the kids are all sorted into social groups like they've been divided that way since birth.

There are a handful of rich kids, the ones who get picked up at the end of the day by Mom or an older brother driving the big new Discovery or Lincoln Navigator. One cut down are all the wannabe rich kids, the ones with the designer clothes but who still have to walk home. Then there are middle groups — the hackers and skaters, the born-agains and beach babes, the jocks and jokers, the kids who'll pleasantly ignore you and those that will beat you up for lunch money ... it's the usual list. But my point is that everybody is in some kind of group, friends with a certain bunch of friends — for life. And that makes it hard to show up for classes just after Christmas, looking like you're about ten years old, and feeling about as confident as anybody who's just been yanked from a decent house and a decent school and a decent bunch of friends and stuck here, nowhere, with nobody, feeling like nothing.

"Stop whining," says Miss P., who immediately made friends with the girl next door. They now have a gang of eight-year-olds who have just gotten beyond Barbie dolls, but not by much.

And really, I don't whine, but I wasn't quite so lucky after the move. Most of the houses on our block were still empty, and none of them had guys my age. I kept thinking, if I could make just one friend, maybe it wouldn't be so bad, but for three months I was just an outsider. A loner. A pasty-faced, freckled kid with an eight-buck haircut who just didn't seem to fit in.

"Jordan Bellemare ... earth to Jordan." I look up. It's the voice of my teacher, Mrs. Marsinello. The kids call her Mrs. Marsbars because that's what she snacks on all day.

"Uh, yeah?" Everybody is staring at me. Smirking. I hate smirking, it's like they all think they're so wonderful and are so happy when they see me screw up.

"Your homework, Jordan."

"Uh, I didn't get it quite finished," I said, which was pretty much the truth. I had done maybe half a question, but Mrs. Marsbars was an all-or-nothing teacher when it came to homework. In her eyes, I'd have done nothing.

Besides, I was helping an old lady bury a quartz head, but I couldn't expect anybody to believe that.

"Not finished?" she asked. "Or not started?"

"His starter went dead," somebody said ... and then there was a giggle at my expense. I heard somebody else say "bonehead" and somebody else whisper "loser."

"I'll have it for you first thing tomorrow," I told her, trying to ignore everyone else.

"No, you'll have it before the day's out, Jordan," Mrs. Marsbars declared, sounding like Judge Judy. "Detention."

Another giggle came over the class. Smiles of satisfaction. Justice had been done — to me, and not to them. That always adds to the enjoyment, when it's somebody else who has to suffer.

So I spent the rest of the day with a detention hanging over my head. We went on rotary after morning math, so I trudged off to science class where we looked at slides of the planets, to our bi-weekly music where Mrs. Schwob kept trying to explain something about melody not being harmony, and then to phys. ed where we had a weird game of broomball which I kind of liked.

In guidance, they tell me that this wonderful education is supposed to outfit me to become a nuclear physicist or a stock trader or a world-famous artist or whatever career I want. From what I see, though, it looks like I'll spend my life cooking burgers at a fast food joint with the skills I'm picking up here.

Anyway, we returned to Mrs. Marsbars' homeroom for the last hour, spent largely with some English worksheets. When the 3:15 buzzer went off, almost everybody raced out the door, but I had to sit where I was. Through the window, I could see the sun shining and — honest — a bird singing in a tree. But I was locked up here until my math homework got done.

"Okay, Jordan, get started," Mrs. Marsbars told me while she was erasing the board. By then everybody in the class was gone except for me and Jessica Norton. Jessica is a half-Native kid who is known for two things: first, she's about the smartest kid in class; second, she wears her hair in really stupid pigtails that various people are always pulling. It's like she has a sign on each pigtail that says "pull me — see what happens." Of course, when people do, Jessica shows them that she can slug as hard as your average welterweight boxer.

I ended up finishing the homework I was supposed to do last night. They were some picture frame problems: given a certain sized picture, and a certain size of mat, how big would the frame be if, etc. etc. These weren't very hard, but there were twenty-five of them! Really, I had the basic idea after three or four, so naturally I started thinking about the bird outside on the tree, and maybe drawing the bird inside one of the picture frames.

"Jordan, you're not working." It was Mrs. Marsbars. She has the eyes of a hawk, despite her thick glasses.

"I'm, uh, calculating."

That got a sigh from Mrs. Marsbars and a snort from Jessica, who was typing at the computer.

So we continued working in the almost-silence. Jessica was clicking at the computer, Mrs. Marsbars was correcting some papers, and I was calculating mathematical picture frames. Then the PA went off, and the office secretary asked Mrs. Marsbars if she'd take a phone call. This seemed to get her all perked up, and off she went. I started looking for that bird outside, but it had flown off.

The tap-tap-tap on the computer stopped. "You have a problem concentrating?" Jessica asked.

"It's too nice a day for math problems." Which was true. The only good thing about the west coast was the weather, which was wonderful when it wasn't raining. Back in Winnipeg, we alternated between freezing winters and mosquito-filled summers, but it was easier to keep your mind on math.

"Yeah, I guess," she said, then typed something into the computer.

"How come you got a detention?" I asked. It seemed a little strange that the smartest kid in class would have to stay after school.

"Not a detention," she said. "I got some work to do. Mrs. M. lets me stay after."

"Some work?" I said, with a kind of half-question mark at the end.

"Yeah, work." Tap-tap-tap.

"What kind of work?" Now it was a real question.

"I'm writing something," she said, still clicking away.

"Like what?"

"A novel."

"You can't write a novel. I mean, you're like what, twelve?" I told her.

"Thirteen."

I was surprised. Jessica actually looked eleven, and about as skinny as my little sister. But she was smart, so if anybody could write a novel, I guess she could.

"So what's it about?"

"Why don't you get back to your math problems. I need to concentrate," Jessica snapped at me.

"I'm just asking. Like what? Abused girl with pigtails gets revenge on her classmates with a lethal something-or-other?"

She stared at me for a second before she said anything. "How about, a real loser moves into town and can't make any friends?"

I didn't blush, really I didn't. But she sure knew how to shut me up.

By the time Mrs. Marsbars got back, I was on problem twenty-three and had gotten pretty sick of picture frames. It was only by some miracle that I managed to get the last two finished. Mrs. Marsbars wasn't paying much attention to me, though. She was reading over Jessica's shoulder, smiling with approval. Must be nice, getting a smile like that when you do something right.

I finally finished up about 4:15, a good hour after school was over, and left the room. I grabbed my jacket from my locker and got my reading-book for homework that night. Then I went down the hall and was dawdling in front of the trophy case when Jessica came out of Mrs. M.'s classroom. We exchanged a look.

"Finish the novel?" I asked. Boy, what a stupid thing to say! No wonder she thought I was a loser.

"Nah. I finished a chapter though," Jessica told me, heading off to her locker.

I felt kind of bad. I didn't know why I was always so sarcastic to everybody. I mean, if I had talked to my old friends like I talked to people around here, well, I wouldn't have *had* any old friends.

Anyway, I was really thinking about that when I walked out the south door of the school. It happened to be at just about the same time that Jessica came and walked out the very same door. I mean, it wasn't as if we were friends or had decided to meet or anything — we just walked through the door at the same time.

But that was enough. The hooting started right away.

Cullen Thurston was leaning up against his brother's car, staring at me and Jessica. He had one of those smirks on his face but he was silent. The hooting wasn't coming from him; it was coming from his buddies Nick and Ryan.

"You two have a good time in there?" Nick asked.

"Look at the new guy's red face — it must have been good. Real goood," Ryan added. My face got redder still.

Cullen just shook his head, superior both to me and to his friends. He was the ultimate cool guy in the school — good-looking enough that he never thought twice about it, athletic enough that every sport came easily, cool enough that anything he did instantly became the thing to do.

Cullen's older brother, Geoff, was behind the wheel of the car, uninvolved. Like Cullen, he was good-looking and cool. Unlike his younger brother, he couldn't be bothered to make fun of an insignificant first-year kid like me.

The two Thurston brothers had nothing in common with Nick. He was fat, ugly and a bonehead in class. If the Thurstons were destined for college, Nick seemed headed right to reform school. He was the kind of guy who really enjoyed making crude jokes or fake farting sounds in class. That was his level.

Ryan was the funnyman in their group, too goofy looking to really belong, but always good for a joke. Ryan wasn't cool, but he was quick and clever and seemed like he'd be fun to know. Still, I think it was Ryan who started the hooting. It was Nick who kept it going.

"She's skinny, but who cares?" Nick shouted.

"Guess you think those pigtails are just *so, so* sexy," Ryan added.

"Gives him something to yank, doesn't it?" Nick replied.

I tried to ignore all this. That's what they tell you, back in that third-grade guidance lesson on how to handle bullies: just ignore them and they'll go away.

Trouble is, the teachers never talk about what happens when you start blushing, when all the blood in your body rushes to your face and turns it some bright tint of pink, or red or crimson. Nor do they say what to do when you stupidly drop your math book on the asphalt. Nor do they tell you what to do when it's been a stinking-lousy day and you don't want to be in this school and you don't want to go home and you have no friends and now a bunch of guys you don't really know are ragging on you.

"Aw, look, he's getting embarrassed," Nick said.

"They only blush when they're guilty, that's what I've heard," Ryan told him. And the two started laughing at me while I tried to pick up the math book.

I don't know why it should take so long to pick up a book when people are looking at you and laughing, but it does. It's soooo slow. You have to reach down and aim at the book, aaaiiim at the book, then grab for it — and miss — and grab again, and then bring it up slowwwwlly because the last thing you want to do is drop it again, because you already feel like a dork and it would be worse to be a double-dork and your heart is already pounding so hard you think it's going to pop out of your chest and lie beating there on the sidewalk.

More laughter. And then the sound of a door closing. I look up and see that Cullen has got inside his brother's BMW and is looking through the open passenger window.

"Aww, leave the kid alone. He's just new," Cullen said.

The laughter stopped. Ryan and Nick muttered something quietly to each other, then got into the back seat of the car.

I made a quick retreat, trying not to look at any of them, trying to will the blood in my face to go back down into the rest of my body where it was needed. Eventually, my blood went back to where it was supposed to be and my face went back to its usual pale white, but not until the Beamer had zipped off down the street and Cullen's friends were just faces in a nightmare.

CHAPTER THREE

A Summer Job

"YOUNG MAHN, YOUNG MAHN!" That's the voice that greeted me when I came around the corner toward my house. I knew right away who it was. Everyone else around here talks with that long "a" sound, so man comes out sounding like *maaaan*. But this "a" was definitely from some old country, someplace.

"Young mahn, I want to talk with you."

Oh, man, I thought, just what I need. She probably wants her silver dollar back. Probably woke up this morning and realized she gave me a silver dollar instead of a quarter and now she wants the money back. But finders keepers, right? Or something like that.

"Yeah?" I said, when I got up to her.

The old lady was wearing one of those Tilley hats, like she had just come off a safari, except with a plastic flower on it, and her white-gray hair frizzed out underneath it. Her skin looked like it didn't see much sunlight, and was about as wrinkled as any I've ever seen. I mean, my grandma has a couple million wrinkles, but this lady had wrinkles in her wrinkles. But the funniest thing about the old lady was that she had on makeup, serious makeup, as if she had to look good for somebody. I mean, when you're that old, what difference does it make?

"Young man, I am so glad to see you," she said.

"Yeah, me too," I lied. Actually, I was a little relieved. She didn't seem angry or upset or anything, so maybe I could keep the money.

"What is your name, what?"

"Jordie. I mean, Jordan Bellemare."

"Ah, you are French, *n'est-ce pas*? *J'habitais à Paris…*" and then she got going with a string of French words that didn't make any sense of me.

"No, no," I broke in. "I don't speak French. It's just, like, my name. My dad's name, that's all."

"Oh, oh, oh. So I understand, yah. Still, you are very nice boy, yah?"

I blushed. What on earth was I supposed to say?

"You work very hard last night, so I see you are good worker. I have job for you, if you want."

"A job?"

"Yah, job."

My jaw must have dropped open. The only job I had done in the last thirteen years was taking out the garbage once a week. Of course, not many kids my age had jobs — but I could have used one. My allowance, when my mom had enough money to give it to me, was all of five bucks a week, less a buck for my so-called education savings account.

"Well, I could use a job, sure," I said. "What kind of work do you need done?"

"The lawn, the garden. You come look."

She took me around so we could look at her front lawn, and the hedge, and the section where she wanted some flowers planted. Then we walked around to the back, where she had already staked out a good-sized garden and, beyond that, a lawn that was almost big enough for a game of football. I was surprised, really, because the lots on our side of the street were pretty small. I guess the builder put the big lots and big houses on the sunny south side and left the north side to us peasants.

"Is a big job, yah? You plant garden and mow lawn. Will be hard work, maybe. But you are big boy."

I smiled at that. I'm not particularly big, just average really, and pretty feeble compared to some kids my age. But I can do garden work. At our old house, before my mom decided I was so hopeless, she had me carrying wheelbarrows full of dirt and rocks all over the place. And I knew how to plant stuff — I mean any idiot can dig a hole in the ground and stick in a flower or a plant. This wasn't going to be rocket science.

"What you think?"

"Piece of cake," I told her.

"What is that?" She looked confused, and it took me a couple seconds to figure out why.

"I mean, no problem. I can do this."

"Good. Come inside, we talk. We make deal."

I followed her in through the back door of the house. On the outside, the place didn't look that much different from my house — a little bigger, maybe, but just the same kind of suburban house that everybody lives in here. But stepping inside the house was like going back into time, like I was in some "Castles of the World" documentary. There were pictures hanging from picture rails on the walls, big moldings at the ceiling and floor, Indian carpets on the floor, and crystal chandeliers in each room. I mean, underneath it all, this wasn't much bigger than our basic house across the street. But somebody had come in and managed to turn her place into a European mansion.

After I got over my initial shock, I started looking at all the *stuff*: porcelain figurines and cut glass paperweights and little statues holding light fixtures and beads and ... it was everywhere. I felt like I was in a museum ... no, I felt like I was in the attic of some museum. The stuff wasn't in any order. The old lady hadn't placed the knickknacks and souvenirs on bookshelves, like my mom does, carefully positioning each piece. She had the junk everywhere, one piece piled on top of another one, some stuff obviously fallen off tables and onto the floor.

"Is a little old-fashioned," she said.

"Oh, I think it's very, uh, elegant," I said. Took me a while to find the word, because mostly I thought the place was a mess, but that was none of my business.

"*Danke*," the old lady said.

"Yeah, right," I replied.

"You like some schnapps? Yah?"

"I, uh, well sure," I said. I wasn't exactly sure what this schnapps thing was. I figured it was some kind of cookie. My grandmother is big on giving us cookies whenever we'd go to see her, or at least she used to, before she moved to an old folks' home.

"You sit, please," she said.

I looked around for some place to sit down, but all the furniture seemed so antique that I thought it might break if I breathed on it too hard. I decided to stand while the old lady went upstairs.

It was after she left that I noticed the ticking. There must have been a dozen clocks all ticking away, from the big grandfather clock by the front window to a tiny crystal clock on one end table. In between there were ticking mantel clocks and glass-covered bronze clocks, clocks in chunks of marble and clocks that were stuck in porcelain figurines. I guess all the windows outside were shut tight, because there was no breeze, no street noise, no nothing. Just the ticking.

It was a little eerie, really. Especially after helping the old woman bury a glass head the night before, I began to feel like I was inside a horror film. This is always the part where the crazy guy comes out of the kitchen with a knife in his hand.

It turned out that the old lady wasn't that crazy. When she came back from the kitchen, there were two glasses in her hand. She handed one to me and I was glad to get it, since I was pretty thirsty from the afternoon, and the walk home, and going around the garden.

"*Skoal*," she said.

I figured this was some kind of old European toast, like cheers, so I said "*Skoal*" too. Then I took a decent-sized drink from the glass.

Whooo! The liquid hit my throat like a rocket, an exploding rocket. I could feel the heat at the back of my throat, then more heat exploding up into my nose and into the back of my brain. I wanted to cough, or sneeze, or something ... but the old lady just stood there, kind of smiling.

"Is better to sip," she said, sipping at hers.

"Ah...yeah ..." I grunted, trying not to cough or puke all over her.

"First, I must thank you again. For the other night, I could not have done that alone. Was too much for an old lady, yah?"

"Well, it was a big rock," I said. "It would have been easier to bury that thing somewhere else, and maybe during the day."

"Yah, but there was no time," she told me. "My son, well, *es ist zu schwierig zu erklären,* how you say, complicated. And is safer under the rock. Better, yah, better. But now, Jordan, we must make the deal," she said to change the subject. "How much you think for lawn and garden, for work?"

I cleared my throat a little and found a voice that I recognized. Mine. "Well, minimum wage, I guess."

"What is that?" she said.

"I, um, I'm not sure," I told her. Actually, I didn't know if minimum wage applied to me since I was underage.

"I have idea," she said. "I pay you one thousand for the work, until end of summer."

"One thousand," I repeated, stupidly. I think I was in shock from the drink, or the amount, or all the ticking.

"Is not enough?"

"No, is enough," I said. I was falling into the same kind of speech that she had, but decided I better stop that. "It's real good." And then I backtracked a little. If I was too excited, she might change her mind. "I, uh, I think that's fair."

"Is deal. You start Saturday."

"Deal," I said. We clinked glasses and I ventured another sip. This one didn't hurt nearly as much as my first gulp.

She reached into the pocket of her dress and brought out a folded bill. I couldn't tell right away what kind of bill it was, but she was handing it towards me so I figured I'd better take it.

"What you say, for retainer. If good, I pay you two hundred each month until fall. Yah?"

"Sure," I said. I figured it would be impolite to unfold the bill, so I just took a peek at it. I hadn't seen one like this before. That meant it wasn't a one or a five or a ten or a twenty. I couldn't figure out what bill it was from the half face that was visible, but I managed to unfold it enough to see the figure in one corner. A hundred dollars. She'd just given me a hundred-dollar bill and all I did was agree to do some garden work.

Whooo! I took another sip, a bigger one, and finished the glass.

"I, uh, you want me to sign something?"

"No, I have your word. Is enough, you are honest boy. I can tell."

"Thank you. Thank you," I said. I felt pretty stupid, repeating myself like that, but what else was there to say.

"No, thank *you*, Jordan."

"Uh, yeah, you're welcome." My name sounded kind of nice with that European accent of hers. "By the way, Mrs., uh … I don't know your name, really."

"I am Mrs. von Loewen," she said, smiling. Her whole face crinkled up when she smiled.

"Mrs. von Loon?"

"Von Loewen," she repeated. "It was my husband's

name, the first one. He was the Count of Loewen, back then, in the old country."

"A count? Like Count Dracula?" I started feeling creepy again.

"No, not storybook count, real count. When I was young and silly, I thought such things mattered."

"So you are, like, Countess von Loewen?"

Now it was her turn to blush. Just a hint of pink came over her white cheeks, and she dropped her eyes. "No, in this country I am just Mrs. von Loewen. Is enough."

CHAPTER FOUR

Cullen's Guys

EVERY SCHOOL HAS SOMEPLACE where kids go to smoke. In the old days, people tell me, they even had rooms inside schools where kids could take a puff. I don't know whether to believe that or not. These days, you can be arrested for holding a cigarette within so many yards of school property, so kids have to sneak away someplace.

The neighbors around our junior high were so watchful that they'd call the cops as soon as the first cigarette butt hit a blade of their grass. So the smokers — all the idiots like me who still puff at the cancer sticks — go off to Ugly George's instead. Ugly George's is not the official name of the restaurant, which is something like Authentic Gyro-Pizza-Donut House, written in small letters just above the big Coke sign. But the kids have given the nickname to the owner, George Papa-something, who isn't all that ugly but doesn't make any effort to make himself beautiful, either.

The really disgusting thing about Ugly George is that, when he's not making a sandwich or selling a donut, he's got a cigarette drooping from his mouth.

Maybe this is why everybody who comes into Ugly George's is a smoker — nobody else could stand it. George tolerates underage smokers, like me, just so long as they order something and don't hang around *too* long.

Anyway, I was in Ugly George's for lunch the day after I got my summer job from the old lady across the street, the countess. What a stroke of luck! So I figured it was time to celebrate. And I had a hundred dollars, at least until I bought lunch and smokes. Only a pack, of course, because I'm going to quit. I was sitting there, finishing my gyro special and feeling pretty good about myself, when Cullen and his friends came through the door. They took a quick look around, not even noticing my existence, and then went over to a booth.

So I finished my lunch, and took out a smoke, and tried to look cool when I lit it as if I'd been smoking for ten years even though I only look like I'm ten years old, so that whole idea is kind of ridiculous. Anyway, I lit the cigarette while Ugly George came over and grabbed the plate, ignoring me, and I was just puffing away when Nick came over to the stool beside me and brought his fat face down to mine.

"Hey, kid. What's your name, anyway?" he said.

"Jordan."

"Listen, Jordan. Since you hang around with Jessica the brain, maybe you got that science homework done."

"Those biology questions?"

"Yeah, them."

"I did them myself," I said, blowing out some smoke, smooth as could be. I may not like math, but I always thought science was pretty cool.

"Well, Cullen needs 'em. Like, we all need 'em."

I just looked at him. I didn't know if this was a shakedown, like maybe there was a threat behind Nick's words, or if he was going to pay me for my answers, or what.

"I said," he repeated, raising his voice and bringing his face closer, "Cullen needs 'em. You get the idea? You'll get 'em back before class, no problem."

"Uh, right," I said. It sounded kind of stupid, but it's what I said.

"So?" Nick demanded.

So I reached into my backpack and found the assignment stuck into the pages of my science book. I pulled out the sheets, looked at them for just a second, then passed them over to Nick.

"Thanks, kid."

"Jordan," I told him, "my name's Jordan."

He didn't even look at me, just loped off to their booth carrying my science answers in his fist like they were a winning lottery ticket.

I immediately felt stupid. Why did I just hand them over? Was I so pathetic that I couldn't even stand up to a jerk like Nick, or so dumb that I actually thought somebody would like me for giving them homework answers? Or maybe I was just so desperate to fit in somehow, with somebody, that I'd do whatever I had to for the privilege.

"Idiot!" I mumbled to myself, leaving the restaurant. I was talking about me, not them, and that's exactly how I felt.

The guys in the booth didn't even look my way when I left, and why should they bother? I was just a pathetic new kid, with a knack for doing science homework.

It took me a while to get over being angry with myself — a boring geography class was enough — and then I realized I might be in bigger trouble. Science class was coming up, the homework was due, and I didn't even have a scrap of paper with my name at the top. I'd been a dork before and now I was about to be a double-dork — I could feel it coming.

The science teacher, Mr. Bartolotti, was an old guy who ran a pretty strict classroom. He even had this sign up behind his desk: No talking, no goofing, no excuses. I sat up near the front, not far from Jessica, while Cullen, Nick and Ryan sat near the back. I kept hoping one of them would come up and drop my answers down on my desk. I was really that dumb.

"Okay, let's have that chemistry assignment," Mr. Bartolotti told the class. "You've had a week on it, so I expect everyone had a chance to complete the work."

He grinned at the class, showing widely-spaced teeth that made him look something like a Muppet.

There was a shuffling of papers as people reached into backpacks and notebooks for their assignments. I opened my backpack and pretended to look inside, all the time shooting looks back to Nick and Cullen. They ignored me.

Mr. Bartolotti went up and down the rows, starting over by the windows, collecting papers as he went. Of course Bob Semele didn't have his done, and Francine the Freckle could only find half of hers. They were like that. When Mr. B. got back to Cullen, he stopped and looked for a second at the sheets Cullen handed him. "Nice job," he mumbled, before moving on to the next row.

Cullen shrugged as if doing the assignment was the easiest thing in the world. I just kept stewing in my own sweat. It took another minute or two for Mr. Bartolotti to reach my desk.

"I, uh, I can't find them, sir," I said.

"You can't find them," he repeated my words, but with a little twist in them.

"No, sir. I had them this morning, right here in my pack."

"But they disappeared," Mr. Bartolotti concluded. "Perhaps it was spontaneous combustion, Jordan, or a disappearance into a black hole. Perhaps your answers had an unanticipated collision with anti-matter." There was a little giggle from the class. "But we don't take excuses here, Jordan. Zero marks for zero work, that's the simple math." He took a pause in his lecture. "I'm disappointed in you."

I was turning red. I hated that "disappointed" line. It was the one my mother always used, so full of guilt and blame. I wish people would just tell you that you screwed up and be done with it. Instead, you get this "disappointed" thing, as if you were personally responsible for ruining their whole day.

"I'll find them," I squeaked out, but he had already moved on.

Through the whole class, I kept waiting for Ryan or Cullen or one of those guys to drop off the answers, but they never did. So I never "found" my assignment and Mr. Bartolotti stayed disappointed. I'd just have to do it over for tomorrow. No big deal, I told myself, I'd had no trouble with it the first time. But all the while I was fuming inside.

When I left school that day, I saw Cullen, Ryan and the rest of them hanging around by the Beamer. I thought about going over and making a big stink about the science assignment, but there were four of them and one of me, and any one of them could pound my face to peanut butter in no time. Best to say nothing, I told myself. Lesson learned. Lesson need not be repeated.

But it wasn't that simple.

"Hey, kid," Nick shouted when I was walking by. "Come on over here."

What now? I thought. Is this homework thing going to become a permanent arrangement? I decided to go over, smile, and do nothing. These guys had made a fool of me once; I wouldn't give them a chance to do it again.

Cullen was leaning against the passenger window. He smiled at me, reached into his pocket and pulled out a pack of cigarettes.

"Here, have a smoke," he said, knocking the pack so one cigarette popped up, just like they do in TV commercials.

"You oughtta give him the whole pack, Cullen," Ryan said. "You owe him."

Cullen shot him an angry stare. "Tell you what. I'll figure out who I owe and what I owe and how much I owe. Me, not you."

There was an awkward silence while Ryan looked down at his feet.

"Here, take a smoke."

"It'll be good for you," Nick laughed, and then began coughing in his smoker's hack.

So I took the smoke. I think my fingers were trembling, but just a little, not so anybody would notice. I reached into my pocket for matches, but Cullen had his lighter out faster than that.

"The answers were good," Cullen told me. "We should all get a good mark."

I couldn't think of anything to say. Was that a compliment? Should I have said thanks, or get lost, or what?

"You're probably wondering why we didn't give 'em back to you," Cullen went on.

"Yeah, kind of."

"Because it was a test," Cullen went on. "We wanted to see what you'd do, whether you'd rat out or what."

"I don't rat," I said.

"Guess not," Cullen agreed. "Of course, you would have been in as much trouble as the rest of us, but you kept your mouth shut. That's good."

"You passed the test, kid," Nick said.

"Yeah, we decided you'd be okay," Ryan joined in.

"Might be," Cullen corrected. "We'll see. Anyway, here's your stuff. Turn it in tomorrow and you only lose ten marks — it won't kill you. And my brother will give you a ride home, if you want."

I looked down at the sparkling red Beamer. It wasn't a new one, of course, but new enough. Somebody had done some work on it, tinting the windows and modifying the wheels. I'd never in my life ridden in a car like that, not once. And here was Cullen, opening the passenger door.

CHAPTER FIVE

Always Be Careful

"SINCE WHEN DO YOU GET A RIDE HOME?" **Miss P. asked** when I got to the house.

She was playing some kind of stupid game with her friends Cindy and Jaz. They were at the front of the house and must have seen me getting out of Cullen's car. I could just imagine the three of them talking about it in their idiot eight-year-old style.

"Since when do you get to ask dumb questions?" I shot back.

"Just that mom might be interested. 'Cuz I might tell her about these friends of yours and you riding in their car." Miss P.'s two buddies laughed at this line. I was looking at a little conspiracy of eight-year-olds.

"You can tell her anything you want, Miss P. I've got a couple things she might want to hear about you and your friends." And then I stomped off to my room while the three girls exchanged giggles and "oohs."

That's what I hate about Miss P. She's a little spoiler, just waiting to shoot down anybody who's feeling good about himself, which sometimes happens to be me.

45

It's not even that the ride with Cullen and his friends was all that great. I mean, we didn't come *directly* to my house, but we didn't spend all that time cruising the streets either. Mostly we just talked, or they just talked and I listened, about some of the cool stuff they did, or were going to do. And we cranked up the stereo real loud for a couple of tunes, one that Nick liked and one heavy metal song that Cullen's brother had to play three times.

Still, it was fun — probably the most fun I'd had since we moved. At least I had somebody to talk to. If there was anything I missed when we came here, it was having friends to talk to. The Internet is okay and all that, but I still think face time beats ICQ time, especially for somebody like me who doesn't type real fast.

I had good dreams that night. I was some kind of Batman, zooming around in a Batmobile that looked a lot like Cullen's brother's BMW. In my dream, I was busy protecting Gotham from some evildoer when I was woken up by scratching at my door. It was Miss P., of course. She scratches because once she woke me up by pounding too hard and I really let her have it.

"Jordie, you got a phone call," she shouted through the door.

"What?" I picked up the phone but there was nothing there except the dial tone.

"From some old lady with an accent. Mrs. von something. She needs you for something."

I opened the door and stared at her. Miss P. looks kind of cute when she looks up at you, but it's the cute look that disguises the real brat. "Like when did she call."

"Early. I was watching cartoons."

I looked at the clock. It was almost eleven. "And you couldn't wake me up to tell me. Thanks a lot."

"Mom said to let you sleep."

"I can't sleep. I've got a job," I told her.

"You?"

"Yeah, me. Your big brother."

Miss P. looked at me with wide eyes, maybe even with some new respect. It's hard to know, really, what's going on inside her head, but I wasn't going to waste any time worrying about her. I figured I'd better hop right over to Mrs. von Loewen's place to see what she wanted.

So in two minutes flat I was knocking on Mrs. von Loewen's door. I was surprised to see her in a kind of artist's smock when she answered the door. As far as I knew, she wore dresses all the time, but now she looked like some kind of painter.

"Oh, Jordan, I am so glad you come. Is too hard for me," she said.

Beyond her I could see a stepladder set up in the middle of the living room. It was directly under a big chandelier.

"Were you trying to change a lightbulb?" I asked.

"No, no. Is a chandelier for candles, you know. But I want to clean crystals, so I get out ladder, but is too hard. I think I am much too old lady for that."

"You're not old," I told her. That was a lie, of course, since she was old enough to be my great-grandmother. She might be pushing a hundred for all I knew. But I learned years ago that old people don't like to be told that they're old, just like little kids don't like being told that they're little. "Here, I'll get it down."

"Thank you, Jordan. You are such good boy."

It actually wasn't so easy getting the crystal thingies off the chandelier. They were hooked on with little bits of wire, and some of those had gotten twisted. I ended up sticking the crystals into my pants until my pockets were filled, so I must have looked pretty ridiculous when I came down the ladder.

"You need help washing them?" I asked.

"No, no. I am old lady, but not helpless old lady. Maybe tomorrow you hang them back up for me. Is extra. I pay."

"Look, Mrs. V," I said, "you don't have to pay me for stuff like this. A little job like this I'm glad to do because ..." I searched for words, but couldn't find the right ones. "... just because," I repeated, kind of stupidly.

"You are very sweet boy. Listen," — I heard a whistle from the kitchen — "I make water for coffee. You wish coffee?"

I thought about it for just a second. I suppose I could have gone home and had some instant breakfast, or bugged Miss P., or watched TV — but why? Might as well sit and talk for a while. "Sure," I said.

I took the crystals from the chandelier out to the kitchen and deposited them into some foul-smelling liquid in a dishpan, then washed my blackened hands.

"You go to dining room, Jordan. I serve the coffee and *apfel kuchen* … I mean, how you say, apple cake."

So I went to the dining room and sat down on these creaky old chairs she had. The dining room table was enormous, like maybe you could get a dozen people sitting at it, and it seemed kind of funny for an old lady living on her own. She must have had a big family, once, or maybe entertained a lot.

It's strange to think about old people back in the days when they had a life, if you know what I mean. You see them hobbling around, puttering in the garden or going to the supermarket for a big outing, and you forget that once upon a time they had little kids and friends, that they drank and smoked and partied. I was thinking a bit about that when Mrs. von Loewen came in with this enormous silver tray.

"You see, I am old but can still serve coffee and cake," she said, putting down the tray. "But now it takes two trips." She went off to the kitchen and came back with an enormous silver coffee pot, almost half as big as she was.

"That must weigh a ton."

"Yah. Is why I can't bring on the tray. Of course, in the old days the lady of the house did not bring the coffee herself. There was help then."

"Help?"

"Maid and, how you say, butter, no, butler is word. When we live in France, there was four, five people to help us. And in Vienna, oh, many more. I was young and strong, but they would let me touch nothing. I did not open window or even pour glass of water for myself until the war. That was the times, then."

"You were rich."

"Everyone was rich. And later we were all so poor, and so many dead. It was terrible, Jordan. I have almost nothing from then except my pearls."

I hadn't really noticed the pearls, since they were underneath her smock, but I could see a couple of them at her neck if I looked.

"Your pearls," I said, making conversation.

"Yah, we had to sneak them out of the old country. My husband, the count, he wanted me to save the diamonds, but I did not care about them. No, the pearls were what mattered. Some I got from my mother. You have heard of Anastasia of Russia?"

"Uh, no," I admitted.

"Well, is no matter. My mother was full of stories and lies. But I have left of those days only the pearls.

Everything else is gone and sometimes, sometimes I am so sad."

"Well, I think you live pretty well," I said, trying to cheer her up. I looked around her house, chock full of knicknacks and keepsakes, porcelain vases and statues, and all the ticking clocks. "And you have a nice chandelier," I said.

"The chandelier was later," she said, "in France. My husband, my second husband, he bought that for me on our, I can't remember, our anniversary. Is good, though, yah? Is not Austrian crystal, but French crystal is good, yah?"

I nodded my head and smiled. I mean, how much did I really care about chandeliers? But the cake looked really good, so I grabbed a slice from the silver tray and took a sip of my coffee, which was very, very strong but drinkable after I added another spoonful of sugar.

"You, Jordan, you remind me of my first husband, the count. You have his eyes, I think. And he loved his *apfel kuchen*."

"It's good," I mumbled, my mouth full.

"The count, he loved his sweets. *Apfel kuchen* and *Sacher torte*. Have you ever had *Sacher torte*?"

"Uh, no," I mumbled. How come people always ask questions when your mouth is full?

"You would like it, I think," Mrs. von Loewen said, with a smile. "But what of you, Jordan? You have history, too, yah?"

My head was kind of spinning. What about me? Nobody ever seemed to ask me that, or wonder about it, or expect very much. I was born back when my mother was still a waitress and my father was, in her words, a "good for nothing" who dropped out of my life when I was three and my mom married Miss P.'s dad. I didn't much like that new guy, and wasn't sad when he left. My mom tells me I still look mostly like my dad, which can't be a very good thing, and not at all like Miss P., for which I am grateful. As for the rest of my life, what was there to say? I felt like I was still waiting for it to start.

"I'm really just kind of ordinary," I told her.

"No," she said, her voice suddenly loud. "No one is just ordinary. We are all special, just special in different ways. Is what you make of yourself that matters. So, what you wish to make of yourself?"

That was a stumper. Nobody ever seemed to ask me what I wanted to do with my life, except school guidance counselors who don't really care what you say back. But Mrs. V.'s question seemed more serious, and I wasn't sure I had a good answer.

"Well, it's kind of dumb," I said.

"Nothing is dumb if you believe in yourself, Jordan. So what is your dream?"

"I, uh, when I was little I always wanted to be a superhero, you know?"

"What is that?"

"These guys who rush around in capes, and they've got superpowers and do heroic stuff against bad guys, like standing up against evil and all that."

"Ah, and so you want to be a hero?"

"Yeah, well, kind of." It sounded so simple when she said it, but still a bit stupid.

"You don't need super powers to be a hero, Jordan," Mrs. V. went on, "just courage. My first husband, the count, he had courage. He was, I think, a hero."

"So what happened to him?" I asked.

"The Nazis killed him. He stood up to them, and they killed him." She looked very far away, or very far into the past. "Is not easy to be hero, no."

"No," I said. "I'm sorry."

"Ach, don't be sorry. Was long, long ago and now life is simple. You are a good boy, Jordan. You can be hero if you want, I think. When the time comes, you will have courage, I can see it."

"I ... I hope so." I was getting a little uncomfortable. I was so used to having my mother tell me that I would end up just like my good-for-nothing father that I didn't know how to handle a compliment. So I decided to change the subject.

"Mrs. von Loewen, that crystal skull the other night?" I began.

"Yah?"

"Well, I was wondering ... why did you want to bury it? I mean, really."

"Because of the curse," she said quietly. "My father, he found the skull in Belize. He told me there was a curse, but I did not believe. But later he would blame it for what happened, so then we kept it in a box, a special box. But when I move here, the movers, they broke the box and ... and I could feel the bad luck coming back."

"But why the big hurry? I mean, you were out there in the dark."

"Well, then there is my son. Sometimes I think Heinrich is a very greedy boy. He does not understand the power of the skull, only what it might be worth." She looked up at me. "I know, I am silly old lady. But I know what my father said is true. And now the skull was telling me it should go back to the earth. And so."

"So that's where it is."

"Yes, where it belongs. We are safe," she concluded.

"So long as it doesn't get mad when I start planting your garden." I laughed at the craziness of all this. Imagine taking a curse seriously! Then again, imagine somebody in a hundred years sticking a shovel in the ground and hitting a quartz skull.

"Just you be careful, Jordan. Even a hero must be careful."

CHAPTER SIX

Initiations

IT WAS ANOTHER TWO WEEKS before I got a second ride in Cullen's car. It was two weeks of pretty hard work in Mrs. V.'s garden and pretty miserable days at school doing other guys' homework and generally sucking up.

So let me tell you, I felt pretty good when Nick said I could go for a ride with them after school. It was a beautiful end-of-May day, the sun was shining and the Beamer's top was down. The only problem with this perfect pictures was that Cullen was sitting in the driver's seat, and he was only fourteen.

"We want to see if Cullen can drive this thing," Geoff told the rest of us.

I was sitting in the back, wedged between Ryan on one side and Nick on the other. We were crowded. Beamers might be fast, but they sure aren't big.

"No problem," Cullen said, gunning the engine a bit too much. Then he shifted the car into gear and we roared out of the school parking lot.

"Hey, hey, I'm too young to die," Ryan said.

"Think I left my guts back there on the street," Nick added.

Cullen was concentrating on his driving. His brother Geoff seemed unconcerned. He tilted his seat back and rolled the window down, checking out some girls who were walking down the street. Then he flashed them a smile, one of those perfect toothpaste-commercial smiles.

"Nice to have a chauffeur," he said, bouncing his head to the music. "Improves the view. But now for a little quiz, Cullen."

"Like what?" Cullen was probably gritting his teeth for fear of smashing up his brother's car — not to mention driving under age.

"Question one," Geoff began, sounding like one of those quiz guys on TV, "the red octagonal object you just passed — it ordinarily means what?"

Cullen swore. "I would have stopped, really. I just didn't see it." And we all laughed.

"That leads to question two. If the cops should pull us over, what do you do?"

"I dive into your seat, like fast, and you get out to talk to the cop."

"Excellent," Geoff told him. "You pass. Now turn right, up ahead, toward Burnaby. I want to check out that new parts shop at the mall."

I have to admit that these guys weren't like the kids I used to know back in Winnipeg. Those guys were sort of goofy and jokey and weird. These guys were so cool that you could catch a social chill from their freezer door, if you know what I mean. Cullen was the guy who decided what was in and what was out, like how you held your smoke, or the kind of T-shirt you wore to school, or even what kind of socks you put on your feet. Needless to say, neither my T-shirts nor my socks nor anything else I wore quite measured up, but I did learn how to hold a smoke properly. At some point, I guess, they decided my homework answers and general sucking up earned me a chance to hang out with them a little ... sometimes. And since the only other person who paid any attention to me at Alex Colville High was Jessica Norton, the aspiring novelist, I didn't have a lot of social options, did I?

So I was real glad when they finally offered me a second ride home. Real glad when Cullen parked the car at the mall so Geoff could go talk to this guy at an auto parts store. Real glad to be leaning against a Beamer and having a smoke in the sunshine with guys like this, especially when two hot girls from school came by and saw me with them. All I needed was a couple of decent shirts and some two-hundred-buck sunglasses like Cullen's and then I'd really fit in.

"So, kid," Nick began when we were on the road again, "I hear you got a job."

"Yeah, well, kind of."

"A kind of job," Ryan snorted. "Like, is it a job or what?"

"Okay, it's a job. I get paid," I said, embarrassed at myself. "There's this rich old lady across the street —"

"Rich? In Ravine Villas?" Geoff laughed. "You gotta be kidding."

"No, really," I said. I was probably turning red in the face. "I don't know why she lives there, but this old lady pays me to do her lawn and help out around the house. And she's gotta be rich — she's a countess."

The four of them all began laughing. Then Ryan came in, "Yes, I am ze Count of Seigel and my sister, Katrine, is ze countessa. Yes, yes."

"And I am ze Duke de Nick, ze, uh, pretender to the throne of, like, Surrey."

And the others all laughed again.

I felt like a fool. No, worse — an absolute, idiotic, total fool.

"But you say she's rich," Cullen said, cutting into the laughter.

"Yeah, I guess," I said, retreating. Last thing I was going to do was to get them all laughing at me again.

"So, like how do you know she's rich?" Nick asked, still grinning at me, just waiting for me to do something stupid.

"'Cause she pays me a lot. And she's got a lot of nice stuff in her house. I mean, you should see all the clocks and things."

"That's okay," Ryan piped up. "I see a clock every

morning when it goes off at seven. What I really need is a baseball bat to smash the thing."

His line got them laughing, and then we started looking at some girls passing by, and then Cullen pulled into this ice cream place so he could switch places again with Geoff. By then, I must have impressed them somehow, or at least reached the point where they were thinking about letting me into the group.

It was Nick who said it, though the idea must have come from Cullen, "I think Jordan's got to get initiated."

"Yeah, we've got to see if he really measures up," Ryan chimed in.

"Initiated? Like how?" I asked.

"Like a test," Cullen replied, casually lighting a smoke and flipping the package so I could grab one. "Remember how you passed the science test?"

"Yeah, like by giving the answers to the rest of us — we *all* passed it," Ryan declared. He thought it was a pretty funny joke, but nobody else joined in with his laughter.

"You see, that test wasn't the real test, if you can follow this," Cullen went on. "The test was how you handled it — whether you stayed cool or you ratted or whatever. And you passed that one; you were cool."

"Passed with flying colors," Ryan said.

"With honors," Cullen agreed, raising the level a bit. "But it was a pretty easy test. The rest of us have all taken tougher tests to be part of the group. You've got to prove that you belong."

"Yeah, even Cullen had to pass a test. Geoff made him rip off a leather jacket from Morrissey's."

"Really?" I said, astonished. I always figured guys like these had enough money to buy whatever they needed. Stealing stuff, well, that was something else.

Cullen nodded. He seemed cold, as if this ancient history weren't particularly important. "The jacket wasn't the point, Jordan," he told me. "Any idiot can rip off a store. In this case, it was the challenge and the chance of getting caught."

"Hey, that guard knew something was up," Ryan said with appreciation. "He almost came after you."

"Almost," Cullen said. "That's the point. You've got to almost get caught — it's got to be that close, but not too close. That's the challenge."

"So what did Ryan do?" I asked. There was a funny lump in my throat, but I figured it was time for me to say something.

"Borrowed a car," Ryan explained. "Thought we should drive a Jaguar for a change. Those Connolly leather seats are just so fine."

"How'd you do that?" I asked him.

"Liquor store. The idiot left it running with the key inside. He deserved to lose the car, really he did."

"But mine was the best," Nick butted in, stealing the show from Ryan. "You ever see the statue outside Haversham's?"

"What's Haversham's?" I asked.

"Yeah, I forget that you're new. So listen, Haversham's is like this really exclusive girl's school, you know, where they wear the kilts and the girls all act like ..." I won't give you the rest of his description, but you can guess. "Anyhow, there's this statue outside on the front lawn of some dancing Greek nymph or something. So I got up there in the middle of the night, hacked the thing off its base, and lugged it away. It weighed a ton, like really."

"But the best part," Ryan said, "was the TV the next day. The Headmistress did this appeal to the kidnappers."

"Yeah, that was us. Kidnappers. And it was just a statue!" Nick hooted.

"So we picked up a reward for giving them their own statue back," Ryan went on. One of Geoff's friends went to pick up the hundred-buck reward. That was the best. That was over the top."

"It was. It was the best," Cullen admitted. "We've tried to top that one, sometimes doing a little dare, a little crazy thing, but nobody's ever topped Nick and the statue. That was heroic."

Nick just beamed. His fat face lit up with pride. I tried to compare him to, say, Hercules slaying the

Gorgon or Terry Fox trying to run across Canada, but the images didn't come together.

"So what about me? What's my test?" I asked.

"Not sure yet," Cullen said. "We're all still thinking. But hang in, we'll let you know. Only one thing I know for certain."

"What's that?" I asked him.

"It won't be easy."

CHAPTER SEVEN

Pool Party

MAY TURNED INTO JUNE, AND I GOT A TAN. This is important only because I had never really tanned before, and it might not have been much of a tan even then, but at least my freckles had turned a little darker. The tan came from my gardening for Mrs. von Loewen. I spent a fair amount of time after school and on Saturdays digging and planting and mulching ... and tanning in the process.

Sometimes I'd plant something in one spot one day and then replant it someplace else the next. Mrs. V. kept changing her mind on things. Finally I started making diagrams of what I put where, so I could keep track of where I'd put the columbines and where I'd put the cornflowers. Mrs. V. had all these gardening books, so I even learned a couple of things about what kind of light a plant or flower needed, and how much water, and what kind of soil. It wasn't rocket science, but there really was a science to it all and I kind of liked it.

When the garden was pretty much started, she got me building one of those garden lattice things, a gazebo or whatever. It's not as if I'm a carpenter — I mean,

I never had a dad to show me how to use a hammer —
but I picked up a couple of things fixing stuff for my
mom. Mrs. von Loewen had all sorts of tools in her basement, so I figured I could use those and follow the
instructions on this kit from the lumber yard. The kit
said it could be assembled in three days, but I was still
hammering away on it for a good two months.

With all the outdoor work, I even had a few new
muscles. I didn't look like a weightlifter, or anything,
but I was filling in my T-shirt sleeves a little better. My
mother said I looked "healthy," which is about as close
as she ever comes to a compliment for me. But I felt
good, had some decent money in the bank, was able to
buy a few cool clothes, and I was finally getting some
friends.

The friends part came hardest. Sometimes I
thought that Cullen and the guys were only using me
for my homework. Sometimes I got mad at the way they
would pick on me or treat me like some kid trying to
make his way into the gang. I guess what bothered me
the most was that Nick kept on calling me "kid" though
I was almost the same age as the rest of them. Once I
told him that. I said, "I've got a name, you know," and
he came back and said, "Yeah, your name is 'kid,' kid."
The others laughed so I just shut up about it.

Still, they gave me a ride home a couple of days
a week. And by June it looked like I had almost been
accepted, except for the "initiation," which they hadn't

decided upon. We had gone shopping and I had bought some swim trunks just like the rest of them, and then Cullen said I could have his old sunglasses so I'd look a little cooler. Ray-Bans. And he gave them to me for nothing.

Anyway, Cullen told me one particularly hot week that I could come over to his place to swim after school the next day when school was let out early for some kind of teachers' union meeting. So on the Wednesday I told my mom I'd be off studying math or something like that, then stuffed my new bathing suit into my knapsack and tried to remember something about the front crawl. I'd wear the Ray-Bans and maybe even look cool, I told myself.

Everything was going along just fine until the second homeroom time before we left for the day. Ryan started telling me this joke, a good dirty one about a doctor and a patient, though I can't remember the details — I never can. Anyway, he got to the punchline at just the wrong moment. Somebody once said that a group of talking people will fall absolutely silent, on average, once every twenty minutes. It's mathematical, really. My problem was that the whole class fell silent just when Ryan got to the punchline and I started laughing. In about two seconds, my laughter was the only noise in the whole, silent classroom.

"Jordan," Mrs. Marsbars barked, "this is quiet group-work time."

"Uh, yes," I said, turning red despite my tan. Then I looked at Ryan and giggled one more time, just a little.

"Looks like you don't quite get the message, Jordan," she said. There was a pause while she looked at the clock and the rest of the class, then the verdict. "The message is ... detention."

"Mrs. M.," I protested while the class snickered. Even Ryan thought it was funny.

"Okay, I'll add another ten minutes. Want to keep going?" she snapped.

I shut up. Her standard detention was twenty minutes, so now I'd be hanging around the classroom for a whole half hour when I was supposed to be swimming. Was this fair or what?

When the buzzer went and everybody else got to head off, Cullen whispered that they weren't waiting around for me. I'd have to walk to his house, about twenty minutes down the road. There wasn't much I could say about it, or much else that could go wrong.

Everybody else left except me, Jessica and Mrs. Marsbars. Jessica began working on her novel, or whatever, and Mrs. M. went off to the office while I sat at my desk. Outside, the sun was shining brightly and a warm breeze was blowing through the two windows that actually opened. There was even the irritating sound of birds outside, chirping away, free to fly and have fun. I was trapped.

"I put you in my book, Jordan," Jessica said, looking over from the computer screen.

"You did?"

"Yeah, I was looking for a kind of pathetic minor character that I can kill off next chapter."

"Nice," I said.

"Don't worry. The alien guns will kill you painlessly, but there will be a lot of your blood and guts all over."

"Sounds great," I muttered.

She paused for a second. I had a sense that she was looking at me. "You know, if you'd choose your friends a little better, you wouldn't get in trouble so much. Those guys are losers."

"And I suppose you're a winner, eh?"

"Not yet, but I will be. And you should take my advice. You know, I kind of like you, at least a little, and nobody else does, not even Cullen and his friends."

Jessica turned back to her computer, Mrs. Marsbars came back into the classroom and I sat there fuming. Imagine Jessica, the ultimate loner, telling me that nobody liked me! I should have let her have it, telling her how stuck-up she was, how everybody thought her "I'm going to be a great writer" pose was so pathetic. But I couldn't say anything with Mrs. M. in the room, and when the teacher let me go before my half-hour was up I didn't stick around to give Jessica a piece of my mind.

It was hot when I got outside. The sun was beating down and you could see the heat coming off the sidewalk in transparent sheets. I started walking toward Cullen's house and was sweaty within the first two blocks. By the time I got to his place, I looked like I'd walked through a thunderstorm, but I didn't smell nearly that good. I tried to wipe some of the sweat away before I rang the doorbell. No sense giving Nick another chance to make fun of me.

I was a little surprised at the house. Somehow I always figured that Cullen and Geoff were rich kids, that they'd have some kind of sprawling house with three garages and a bunch of cars in the driveway. But this house wasn't much bigger than mine and didn't seem very impressive at all, just your basic suburban house, except it had a pool out in back.

I rang again after a minute or so. I could feel the cool air conditioning inside leaking out the bottom of the door, but nobody came to open it. Still, I could hear some music and shouting from around the back, so I went over to the side fence and opened the gate. If the Thurston family had a Rottweiler, I was about to become supper.

They didn't. I walked around back and found all of them at the pool. And they had company — three hot girls from Geoff's senior high school.

"Hey, Jordan! Marsbars finally let you go," Ryan yelled.

"Nah, he wanted the detention so he could spend time with Jessica," Nick said, and got a laugh from Ryan.

"Get your suit on, Jordan. Time to cool off," Cullen shouted from his end of the pool.

He pointed at this change room which seemed to be built onto a shed where the pool pumps and filters did their work. I went into it, stripped off my sweaty clothes and put on my bathing suit, stuffing my clothes into the knapsack with my books. Outside the shed was a little shower, and I figured that would be a good idea to use it, given the sweat from my walk. What I hadn't figured was how cold the shower would be. I knew better than to shout, but I didn't stay under the showerhead very long.

The water felt good after I jumped in. It was relatively warm, at least compared to the shower, and I really could swim a little, at least enough for a backyard pool. I swam from the cabana end of the pool over to where Geoff was talking with the three girls. I tried not to stare, really I did.

I was floating back to the other end when I heard Geoff say something about me. I couldn't quite get the words — something like "poor kid from nowhere" — but the tone indicated that I was something pretty pathetic.

I climbed out of the other end and was met by Ryan. "So what did you get for laughing at my joke?"

"Only twenty minutes," I said, drying off. "She let me go early."

He turned and looked in the only sensible direction. "You see the girls?"

"Yeah, I got eyes."

"Nice, eh?"

Actually, they were gorgeous. Two of them were in one-piece suits and one of them wore a bikini. They were all hot, but the last one had the kind of body that bikinis were made for. "Yeah, real nice. They going out with Geoff or what?"

"Think so, one of 'em. The other one has her eyes on Cullen. And the funny-looking one is my sister Kathryn." He pointed at the girl in the bikini. I'd heard that Ryan had a sister in tenth grade. What amazed me, given that Ryan was so goofy-looking, was that his sister was gorgeous.

"She's sure not funny looking."

"Yeah, but she's my sister. That makes her weird, by definition."

Ryan took me over to meet the girls, despite everything I said about not being interested and just wanting to swim. Ryan knew it was just a cover-up, and so did I. The truth is that I was terrified to be so close to three hot girls.

They didn't seem nearly as awkward to be close to me. "So you're the kid," said the tallest one, flipping her long hair back over one shoulder.

"Uh, yeah. My name's Jordan," I said back.

"Nice tan, Jordie," the dark-haired one told me, sarcastically.

"Come on," said the tall one, "I like that T-shirt-tan look. It's so country music, or something. Like the kid just got off a tractor."

"Ewwh!" said the dark-haired girl. "That is way too gross." The way they were talking, it was almost as if I wasn't really there

"C'mon," Ryan's sister Kathryn said, "I think he's kind of cute."

"Yeah, but he's got to learn how to talk to girls," the tall one went on. She was looking at me, trying to catch my eyes, which were staring down at my feet … kind of. "Hey, kid, my eyes are up here, right? Up *here*!"

Then the three of them burst into giggles while I stood there, turning a bright shade of red. It wasn't sunburn.

"Hey, be nice to the kid," Nick said, attracted by the laughter. "He just looks like that cuz, well, he looks like that."

"My name is Jordan," I repeated, almost spitting out the words.

"Hey, guy, no offense," Nick muttered.

"Hey, did you guys hear that Jordan makes big bucks working for some countess in Ravine Villas," Ryan said, changing the subject. I owed him big time for that.

"A countess?" said the tall one, unbelieving.

"Really?" asked Ryan's sister. "That would be too cool."

"She is a real countess, Countess von Loewen," I said, trying to sound as Germanic as I could. "Her husband was a German count, but she lived in France after the war."

"In Ravine Villas?" asked the dark-haired one. "Did she wander away from her castle, or what?"

"I don't know why she lives there," I told them. "She's got money, enough money to pay me for yard work and building stuff. And the house is pretty nice."

"Pretty nice," Ryan said. I could see him getting powered up for a joke. "Does that mean the kitchen has the deluxe Formica, or what?"

The girls laughed again. Everybody was looking at me. I reached up and wiped away some water or sweat from my cheeks, not sure what to say.

"Well, it's a nice house, inside. There's this chandelier from France, for instance."

"Sounds like Martha Stewart," the dark-haired girl commented. "Does she offer tours of the garden ... or does the staff take care of all that?"

"Jordan is the staff," Ryan declared, and everyone laughed.

I tried to ignore all this. "Listen, it's true. She's got all kinds of weird stuff all over the place, clocks and porcelain doodads and all this old world junk. But the best thing is this head made out of crystal or something."

"A head?" somebody said.

"The old lady's got a head?" Cullen asked sarcastically. "I should hope."

"Excuse me while I go use the head," Ryan threw in.

And then the comments came at me, like a missile barrage: "Nice head." "I'll show you a head." "Maybe a stuffed head." "Is it a live head or what?"

"No, it's a quartz head ... a skull, really. It's from South America," I said, trying to cut them off. "Her father got it years and years ago. There's this curse on it, but it's probably worth a fortune."

Cullen suddenly got interested. "A quartz head ... like crystal quartz?"

"Yeah."

"How big?"

"Almost life-size."

Cullen looked over at Geoff, and then at Nick. There was some kind of silent conversation going on between the three of them, but I didn't get it at the time. All I got was the attention of the girls, who wanted to know if Mrs. von Loewen had jewelry or booze or what. I couldn't figure out what business it was of theirs, but I made up answers anyhow. I said that Mrs. V. had a wine cooler and a huge liquor cabinet and a secret safe full of jewelry. I mean, they'd never be able to check it out, so I just let my imagination go wild.

So I was bragging away, paying no attention to the guys — and that made me an easy target, standing where I was at the edge of the pool. Nick came charging at me, his shoulder smacking into me full force.

I went flying, face forward, right into the pool. I flailed a little as I hit the water, then glugged my way back to the surface. The stunt got everybody laughing, and in a couple of seconds everybody was throwing everybody else in the water — sunglasses and all. Soon all of us were floating around, laughing and splashing.

Need I mention that I had a great time that afternoon. No, I had a GREAT time, the capitals do it better. We floated and sunbathed and joked and pigged out on salsa and chips and laughed until the sun was almost setting.

At the end, I was towelling off, getting ready to put my clothes back on, while the other guys were off talking among themselves. Maybe that's why I found myself alone with Ryan's sister Kathryn.

"You know, Jordan, you're kind of fun," she told me.

"Really?" I said. For a second I was afraid I was being set up.

"Yeah, really. I can see why my brother likes you. My friend Janey thinks you're kind of cute, too."

"She does?" I was astonished, really astonished.

Kathryn just grinned and walked away, and I was left feeling pretty good about myself for a while. It was one of those moments when the sun is shining, not just outside, but inside.

That's just when Cullen came up to me. He smiled with the news, "We've come up with it, Jordan. Your initiation."

"You have?"

"Yeah, and it shouldn't be too hard. Remember that skull you were talking about, the one that the old lady's father found? Well, we want you to bring us the skull. We want to see that there really *is* a skull, if you know what I mean."

"But ..." I hadn't told them that I'd buried the skull under a large stone and a lot of dirt.

"No buts, I'm afraid." He was still smiling, still polite. Cullen was always like that, cool and smiling, but with an edge just beneath the surface. "We have a few doubts about you and so the skull will tell us if you're solid or not. Just bring it to us and you're in. Otherwise ..."

He didn't have to finish. The otherwise meant "you're out" or "it's been a slice" or *hasta la vista* — there are lots of phrases for the same idea. I knew all too well what it meant to be an outsider, and I didn't want to go there again.

A Gift

"YOU'RE AN IDIOT, YOU KNOW THAT?"

Jessica was sitting at the class computer, working on the novel that everybody knew she'd never finish. Nick had told me that she started working on some kind of family history back in grade five and never really got that finished, at least that anybody knew. But a year later Jessica actually got a story published somewhere, in some kind of contest, and decided that she was the next Alice Walker, about to be discovered as soon as her big "novel" was finished. Mrs. Marsbars humored her, but everybody else laughed at her behind her back. The great *writer*, the grand *artiste*! That's what Ryan would say, and then we'd all laugh. Here she was, calling me an idiot! Like, riiight.

"Okay, maybe not an idiot," she went on despite my silence. "You're naïve. You're so naïve you can't even see straight."

"Yeah, sure," I grumbled, plugging away at the fifth-last geography question. "Like, what don't I see?"

"That Cullen and those guys are using you."

"Yeah, sure," I grunted, ignoring her. I was doing another page of math problems. I had gotten better about my homework, really I had. But the night before, Cullen invited me over for a swim again and told me that Kathryn would be there with a *new* bikini. I mean, how important was a math drill sheet, anyhow? So it was worth a detention.

What did Jessica know, anyhow? Friends are always using each other. That's what it means to count on people — that they're there when you need them. My friends could count on me for some homework help. I could count on them for a swim in Cullen's pool, or a ride home, or a chance to see Ryan's sister. That wasn't *using* each other. It was trading off. Right?

"You keep on hanging with them and you're going to end up in trouble. You're getting sucked in. You even wear their clothes now."

That last part was just because I had borrowed one of Cullen's sweatshirts and we had switched running shoes a couple of days before. Actually, I hadn't really spent much time with the guys since the pool party. They were waiting to see how I'd handle the initiation.

I guess I was wondering how I'd handle it, too.

"Why do you care so much?" I asked her.

"'Cause I thought there was some hope for you, Jordan. I thought maybe you were okay. But I must have guessed wrong."

"Guess so," I said, trying to act just as bored as I possibly could.

I'd been getting a lot of grief for hanging out with the guys. My sister, you can imagine. "That Nick is soooo disgusting, blah blah blah." Even my mother, who had never before paid much attention to my friends, seemed to have some kind of problem with Cullen. "Where does his brother get the money for a car like that?" she asked one night.

"I don't know," I told her, which was the truth.

"It's an expensive car for a kid to drive, isn't it?" she went on.

"Yeah, I guess." I was waiting for her to come to some point, and I didn't have to wait long.

"Jordan, listen, it's more than just the car," my mom said. "You've changed since you started hanging out with those kids."

I felt like telling her that I had something on my mind, like how to get a cursed quartz head out of the ground, or whether I should, or whether I should go back to being a nobody. But that was all too complicated, so I said, "Changed? Like how?"

"'Like' your attitude," she said. "Sometimes I'm not sure I even know you anymore."

Well, you could spend a little more time trying to talk to me, I thought. But I didn't say that; I didn't say anything.

"You seem to hang out with these new friends all

the time, or else you're over at Mrs. von Loewen's."

"This house is to small to hang out, Mom. There's no air conditioning, and Cullen's got a pool."

"That's not what I mean," she said. "At least for Pris, I know the girls she hangs out with. And I used to know your friends back in Winnipeg, and their families. But not these guys."

"We're not kids anymore, Mom."

"You're just thirteen."

"Almost fourteen," I corrected. "I'll be driving in two years."

She stopped for a second and went to the freezer, pulling out some frozen breadsticks. For a second, I thought the inquisition was over, but I was wrong.

"Just stay put," my mom ordered. She put the breadsticks on a tray and popped them into the oven.

"Jordan, ever since you started seeing those guys, you've been walking around here with a chip on your shoulder, an attitude that I just don't like."

"Right," I said sarcastically.

"See, you're doing it again. And your marks aren't what they used to be, either. I had a call from Mrs. Marsinello about you not doing homework last week. I thought we got over that problem."

I should have figured that Marsbars would be behind this.

"It was just once. And the school year's almost over."

"It's not just once, Jordan," she said, her voice cracking a little. "It's like it was back when we first moved, before you got your job with Mrs. von Loewen."

"Well, it wasn't my idea to move here, was it?" my voice was rising. I knew that I was getting red in the face, too.

"Don't talk to me like that, young man," she scolded. "I had an offer for what I thought was a good job, so I took it. We do what we have to do."

"Well, so do I. And I like hanging out with my friends. What's so weird about that?"

"We do what we have to do," my mother had said. She was talking about her own problems, of course, but maybe her words would work for me. The guys wanted the quartz skull; they wanted some kind of proof that I deserved to be in the group. And who would it hurt if I dug the thing up and took it over to them? Mrs. V. didn't want it; she was the one who had me bury it. Nobody else even knew the thing existed, except maybe her son, so who would be hurt?

"Do what you have to do," I told myself.

Except something in my gut didn't feel quite right about it. The skull wasn't mine; it belonged to Mrs. V. If the skull did have a curse, digging the thing up wasn't helping anybody. And what kind of guys would ask me to steal something to prove I deserve to belong? I mean, was I that desperate?

The other thing was, Mrs. V. was always so *nice* to me. Frankly, I preferred going over to her house because nobody there would bug me, not like my mother or Miss P. or even Nick. When my work was done, Mrs. von Loewen would bring out some strudel or Linzer torte or some other rich dessert, and that thick coffee or sometimes some schnapps — and then she'd tell me how wonderful I was.

It was so unlike my house, where nothing I ever did seemed to turn out right and nobody ever talked to anybody else. Mrs. V. liked to talk — I mean, she'd tell me these stories about the old country and her sons and these places she used to live. And she also liked to listen. So I would tell her about Mrs. Marsbars or school or what I learned about plants and flowers, and she'd nod her head and only sometimes fall asleep. Still, it was a lot better than my house where nobody would even pretend to listen.

And Mrs. V. kept doing nice things for me. Not just the regular pay and the bonuses for extra work, but nice things. I remember near the end of June we were sitting out on the back patio. We'd been talking for a while about something or other, and then Mrs. V. looked at me. I mean, she *really* looked at me.

"Jordan, Jordan, you are getting such a big boy."

"Not so big," I said.

"Yah, big," the countess said in her funny accent. "Big muscles. And you are getting mature, too, I think." She said mature so it came out like "ma-toooor."

"Really."

"Yah, there is hair on your face now. Soon you will have mustache, then beard. It think maybe you would be good with a mustache, yah?"

"Well, it's not really cool," I said. "And mine would be blonde."

"Then I guess you will have to shave," she said, and suddenly her whole face lit up. "Yah! Perfect! I get you something." Then she went running off into the house.

It was funny to see her move fast. Her legs were kind of skinny and she walked strangely, with one leg dragging a little. The guys told me they'd seen her once or twice and thought she looked loony. I just told them she dressed like a countess from before the war, which is exactly what she was.

"Here, here. I found it," Mrs. von Loewen said when she came back. She was out of breath from her run into the house.

"What is it?" I asked. She handed me a velvet-covered box, about the size of a hardcover novel.

"Open. Is yours," the countess said proudly.

I opened the lid and saw a razor — a silver razor like they used to have ages ago. Along with it were some blades, the old two-sided variety, and a container of shaving soap — not shaving cream, but a bar of soap.

"It's a shaving kit," I said.

"It was my husband's ... the count. Now I give it to you."

I wasn't sure what to say. It was a fabulous gift. The razor was beautiful and weighed a ton. I mean, it would be worth a lot of money if it were melted down ... but as an antique it might be worth a fortune.

"Oh, I can't take this," I said.

"Yes, you must. I insist," she said. Sometimes she sounded very much like a countess.

"But your sons..."

"One is dead. One is ... well, he does not value such things, only what things are worth. No, is for you, Jordan. You are the son I always wanted but did not have. You should get this. The count, he would want it that way."

CHAPTER NINE

Presenting the Skull

So ask me how I felt digging up the skull. Ask me.

But I didn't really have much choice, did I? I mean, I had bragged about the skull and Cullen's guys had called my bluff. If I didn't deliver, they'd drop me altogether. Even worse, they'd pass out the word that I was a liar, a guy who just made up stories to try to seem important. Not only wouldn't those guys be my friends any more, they'd make sure I didn't make any others. I'd be a fool, a liar, a pathetic nobody.

It wasn't that digging up the skull was hard. I simply went out to the front of Mrs. V.'s house, pretended I was replanting a hosta from the back, and dug down where I knew the skull was buried. Mrs. V. never watched what I did. Besides, the front curtains were always closed so she couldn't really see me. I just dug until I hit the stone, then used the shovel to wedge the stone up, and pulled up the burlap sack. I didn't open it. I just grabbed it, tried to carry it as innocently as I could over to our garage, and put it behind a recycling box. Then I went back to fill in the hole.

Dirt. I used dirt to fill in the hole. And I felt like dirt.

Of course, I made all sorts of excuses to myself. Mrs. V. had buried the skull, so she really didn't care that much about it, and it was almost like garbage. I was just recycling garbage, I said to myself. And then I thought that the skull was like lost treasure, and I was a treasure hunter, doing something like archeology to unearth an ancient treasure. And then I told myself, if I had asked Mrs. V. she would probably have said, "Yah, go ahead and take it away, it's yours," or something like that — except that she really did think there was a curse on the thing and wouldn't want the curse to fall on me. So of course I didn't ask; I just dug.

Excuses are easy. Your head just spins around with arguments and ideas, and you can talk yourself into almost anything. But somehow your gut knows. Your gut tells you what you really did.

"Jordan, you look … not good."

I was out in the backyard, working on Mrs. von Loewen's gazebo. The sweat was pouring off me like crazy, though I hardly ever sweat. But it was the pain in my gut that was really getting to me.

"I think my stomach is off a little," I said, without looking up.

"Is not good, your stomach?"

"No, usually it's fine. It's just … I don't know."

"Ach, you work too hard. You rest; I make some ice tea. Yah?"

I looked up. "Yah," I repeated.

I hadn't worked well that afternoon. Half the nails I hit went in crooked and had to be pulled out. Maybe the stupid gazebo kit had come with cheap nails. Or maybe I was having a bad hammer day. Maybe that was it.

"Here, this will help," Mrs. V. said when she returned with the iced tea.

I looked up at her and saw that she was smiling. Her gums had receded so far that her teeth seemed enormous, like those on the quartz skull. Don't think about it, I said to myself. Do what you have to do.

"The gazebo, it will be so wonderful."

"It's not done yet," I said.

"But I can see, already, in my mind. You have made this garden into, what is word, master-thing."

"Masterpiece?"

"Yah, masterpiece. Is so beautiful. I am so proud."

So I should have felt good, really. I should have gotten embarrassed from the compliment, but instead I had this bitter taste and I felt cruddy.

"Maybe I better just go home and lie down," I said. "I'll come back when I feel better."

"Like me, you take nap. Is good."

I smiled and handed the empty iced-tea glass back to her. I really did feel bad, so I was glad to get back across the street and collapse on my bed. Everything seemed to be spinning for a while, and then it stopped.

I must have slept for some time. When I woke up I found myself staring at some old photos on a bulletin board next to my bed: me and Miss P. and my mom. There was one of me and my sister playing happily on the swings that were behind one of our Winnipeg houses. That seemed like a long time ago, before we moved. Before we grew up.

It's funny that you can only remember back so far. I don't remember hardly anything about being a baby. I know I had a father back then. He stuck around for a couple of years, and I've seen pictures, at least a couple that my mother didn't chop up. I remember a little bit about him, just a couple of fuzzy images in my mind, like photographs where the camera couldn't figure out where to focus.

I remember crayons, for some reason. I think once he bought me some special crayons with those colors you don't usually get – you know, flesh tone and military green and all those. I remember the crayons and my dad being so pleased with himself and me being so happy. Last year I asked my mom about it, but she said my father never bought me anything, that he was just a jerk. I don't believe that. But I don't remember enough to know what to believe about him. Maybe he was a count or a prince and just gave up on my mother as too ordinary, too common. I could understand that.

My mom is nothing special. The only thing about her, really, is that she's a bit wingy. Maybe the nice word is "impulsive." She does things like chop up pictures, or throw out all the glasses in the kitchen because a couple are cracked, or burn my socks in the barbecue because they're a little dirty. I love her anyhow, of course. I mean, a person has to love somebody and it sure isn't going to be my bratty little sister, so I guess it's my mom for me. By default. She's all I've got. But lately I know I don't treat her all that well. We seem to have fights about almost everything.

"Jordan, where are you going?" It was after supper and I wasn't feeling much better, but I had told Cullen that I'd be over that night.

"Cullen's."

"You're spending far too much time over there, Jordan. Exams are coming and you should be studying."

"I don't have any homework tonight, Mom. And exams are still two weeks off. There's lots of time to study."

"You'd better study, young man, or it's summer school."

"Would you just stop ragging on me," I shouted. "I'm doing fine, just fine."

I didn't wait for her to say anything else. I stomped out of the house as if I were really mad, then went out to the garage and took the burlap sack from where I had hidden it. I dusted off the dirt, then untied the top and pulled the skull out.

The quartz felt strangely cold, even on a hot day, and the skull seemed to catch whatever light there was in our gloomy garage. It almost looked like it was glowing, though I know it was just the way quartz refracted light. Still, it was kind of spooky. I was staring at this cold, glowing skull in my hands … and it was staring back at me, its empty eye sockets peering into my head or my heart. I shuddered. Quickly I put the skull into my gym bag, then covered it with an old T-shirt.

When I left the garage, I was covered in sweat. I figured I was probably still a little sick from whatever had put me off in the afternoon. Still, it was Saturday night and I had promised to bring the skull. Cullen had said we'd have a party to celebrate and I was looking forward to that. I wondered if Kathryn would be there and what she'd think of the skull. And me.

Anyway, when I got to Cullen's house the place was mostly dark. It turned out that everybody was downstairs, watching an Austin Powers video, and gradually getting drunk. A case of beer was open on the floor and half the bottles had already been emptied.

But there were no girls, just the usual guys and one more I didn't know. I suppose the look on my face showed my disappointment.

"The girls couldn't come," Cullen announced matter-of-factly.

"Hey, Jordan, don't look so sad. We know you got the hots for Kathryn," Nick grunted.

Ryan took a swig of beer and almost spat it out at the mention of his sister's name. "Trust me, you'd be better off with Jessica, the brainer."

"Except for the bod," Nick said. "Jessica's got no bod, but your sister, guy, is one hot babe."

"Would you just shut up," Ryan snapped back. For a second, I thought he might actually jump up and take a swing at Nick, but Cullen intervened.

"Hey, hey, easy," Cullen said in his soothing voice. "No problems, no worries. Besides, I've got to introduce Jordan to the new guy. Mordock, this is Jordan. He's about to pass initiation."

"Hey there," Mordock said. I assumed that had to be his last name, but who knew? He was a pretty ordinary-looking guy, with maybe a few more earrings than usual and a slight scar on his cheek, like maybe once he'd been cut by a knife. He sat on the couch in jeans and a beaten-up leather jacket, looking almost as cool as Cullen.

"So let's see it," Nick demanded.

"The head," Ryan chanted, "show us the head!"

Mordock looked curious but said nothing. Cullen had already seen the way I was holding the gym bag, so he must have known what was inside.

"You know, this wasn't easy to get," I said, unzipping the bag.

"Yeah, yeah, yeah," Nick said. "Now let's see it. Zee skull from zee Amazon!" He started giggling, probably already drunk.

I ignored the sarcasm and reached into the bag. The skull was still cold, and a bit slippery as I tried to grab it. The others suddenly grew quiet, waiting.

Finally I pulled the skull from the bag and turned it so the face looked away from me and at all of them.

"Holy ...." Nick said. And that was all. There was a strange silence as the skull looked at them and they stared back. The basement suddenly felt very, very cold.

"Where's it from?" the new guy asked.

"From this old lady I work for. Her father found it in Belize," I told him. So long as I held the skull in my hands, I felt like I was in control. There was a funny feeling of power that came with it. I can't explain the sensation, I just felt it.

"Hey, hand it here," Nick demanded.

"You sure you want to touch it?" I asked, grinning at him just as the skull was grinning. "There's a curse."

"I don't believe any of that ..." and I'm sure he didn't. I would have handed it to him, but Cullen intervened.

"No, it comes to me first," Cullen ordered and I handed it over. "This is truly, truly ... strange."

He handed the skull to Nick, who was silent for the first time in his life, and then Nick passed it to

Ryan, who couldn't even think of a joke. The new guy wasn't allowed to touch it.

"I've got to give you some credit," Cullen told me. "I didn't believe that there really was something like this, and then I didn't think you'd have the guts to bring it here. You're in, Jordan. No more doubts."

I blushed. I guess I felt some kind of pride. I'd passed my test.

"And you, Skull," Cullen said, talking to the head, "I don't believe in curses, except the verbal kind, so don't look back at me like that." Then he laughed, a big laugh, to show that he was the only person in the room who wasn't spooked.

"Hey, I got an idea," Ryan said. "Put the skull on the shelf under the TV. The thing can watch us while we watch a few videos. I've brought some you'll like, Jordan."

So Cullen put the skull on the shelf, and I looked at it sitting beside the VCR. Something about all this was so weird — so funny but so serious all at once, that I thought I had to do something. Something totally cool.

Then I had a flash. It was simple, really. I went over to Nick and grabbed the baseball hat off his head. Then I tightened the band a little so it would fit, and put it neatly on the skull.

"Look at that," the new guy said, "the skull is a Yankees fan!"

CHAPTER TEN

A Garden Party

MRS. V. NEVER NOTICED that the soil where she'd buried the skull had been dug up. I thought about telling her that I'd borrowed the skull, but I always chickened out. Besides, I told myself, I'd get the skull back in a week or so and bury it one more time. What difference would it make?

Besides, Mrs. V. kept telling me what a wonderful "young mahn" I was so it would have been hard to say anything that would mess that up. I couldn't just tell her, "By the way, you know that skull you buried to stop an ancient curse, well it's sitting in a guy's family room wearing a baseball cap. Sorry." I kept my mouth shut and let my stomach grumble.

My stomach kept grumbling while I finished up the gazebo for her back garden. I really hadn't done all that great a job, but the thing stood up okay and looked pretty good even if some of my cutting and hammering was a little iffy. Mrs. V. thought my almost-finished gazebo was about the best thing built since the Eiffel Tower and decided to celebrate.

"We have garden party, Jordan. Just small one. It will be like old days."

"Sure," I said.

"You are the builder so will be guest of honor. Perhaps your mother and sister will come. Your sister, she seems very nice, yah?"

"Whatever you say," I replied.

"And your mother, I think she works so hard for you. You must be nice to her, Jordan. You are nice, aren't you?"

"Yes," I lied, and felt guilty about that too. I felt guilty about lots of things lately, though my treatment of my mother was the least of these.

It took a while to get everything fixed up for the garden party. The countess put me to work polishing silver and planting flowers and buying more flowers at the store. She wanted the garden fixed up just perfect- ly for the big event.

And she wanted me fixed up, too.

"Now you must smile when you are introduced, Jordan," she said.

"I know, I know."

"You practice. Now you shake hands with me, and smile, and say 'how do you do, Mrs. Jones.'"

"But you're not Mrs. Jones."

"Is practice. Now don't be silly, you must practice."

Sometimes Mrs. von Loewen can sound a bit bossy. But she really was my boss so I went ahead with what she wanted. "How do you do, Mrs. Jones," I said.

"More smile. And shake hands with more muscle. Men and women shake hands same way now."

"How do you do, Mrs. Jones," I repeated, smiling more, shaking hands harder.

"*Gut*. You are the guest of honor, Jordan, so you must be gracious."

I blushed. I didn't deserve this, for more reasons than I could explain.

"But you must not say anything about the old days," she told me. "That is my rule."

"So nothing about the count and Europe and all that?"

"Yes, my rule. This is new country so we do not dwell on the past. Besides, people think I am, what is word, upsee, if I use a title."

"Uppity."

"Yes, that word. I do not want to be uppity, just friendly. So you call me only Mrs. von Loewen, okay? No countess. It will be better."

Everything was ready for the Saturday afternoon party. Even the weather cooperated. The sun was shining and the air was at that perfect temperature we don't always get in June. The garden looked great. The new plants gave it all sorts of color and the hostas I planted around the base of the gazebo looked good. In fact, things seemed to be growing better since I had gotten the skull out of the ground, but maybe I was just getting superstitious.

The food came from a catering place that Mrs. V. found in the phone book. They brought in platters of those little sandwiches and cookies and fruit. There were carafes filled with wine and bottles with the countess's favorite drink, schnapps. There seemed to be enough stuff to feed a small army, or at least a platoon or two. The house looked great, too, with the crystal all shining and Mrs. von Loewen's antique silverware sitting out beside piles of linen napkins.

Mrs. V. was all dressed up in this old-fashioned dress with lacey swirls that looked kind of Chinese to me. Just the day before, she had gone out to get her hair done so the white curls were all in place. And she was wearing her pearls, of course, big pearls in a long strand that she swirled around her neck several times. She looked great, for a really old lady.

We had a pretty good turnout, too. Mrs. V. had invited people from her church, some neighbors from her old house and a bunch of other people she knew. Mostly it was a pretty elderly crowd — lots of women with white hair and men in blue blazers and shiny white shoes — but they were all nice people.

"Now this is elegant," my mother said when she

came across the street with Miss P. They were both quite dressed up for the occasion, Miss P. looking like one of those kids you see on TV shows that feature little kids singing or tap dancing. Even my mother had unpacked a nice dress, one that I hadn't seen since the days when she was trying to impress my former stepdad.

"Can I have some of that bubbly stuff from the fountain?" my sister asked.

"No, young lady, you stick to Coke. And you, too, Jordan."

I rolled my eyes.

"So that's the gazebo you've been working on," Mom said, changing the subject.

"Yeah. It came in a kit so all I had to do was follow the instructions," I said.

"Well, you did a good job," my mom told me. "You should be proud of yourself."

Which I was, mostly, though it was still pretty amazing to get a word of praise from my mother. I probably blushed, but with my new tan it wouldn't have shown.

Just about then, Mrs. V. started clinking on her punch glass and a bunch of the other old folks did the same. I guess this was some kind of old-world custom for getting people's attention. When the crowd was all looking her way, Mrs. V. started a little speech.

"Is wonderful to have all of you here, here in my new house," she said. "And you see this garden and this gazebo, yah, is all because of a very wonderful young man."

My mom looked at me. Now I was blushing big time.

"Does she mean you, Jordie?" Miss P. whispered. I wouldn't give her an answer.

Mrs. von Loewen went on, "Now that I am getting a little older, as some of you know, is hard to do many things myself. So I have a young man who plants the garden and builds this wonderful gazebo. And I would … I would like to give a toast to him. To Jordan, who is so very, very nice to this old lady."

"To Jordan!" some of the people shouted, and then there was the clinking of glasses and everybody looked at me. Oh no, please don't make me give a speech, I thought, and nobody did. They went back to talking and eating and having a good time.

Later, when the crowd died down a little, we got organized into two teams to play charades, which was something I'd never done before. It's not hard to figure it out though, and I found that my mom was even pretty good at it, and her team won.

By dinnertime, the older people were getting a little tired and filtering out the door. People said their good-byes and took piles of food with them. My mom had taken Miss P. home, so really it was just the countess and me left at the very end. We were both tired.

"Tomorrow we clean up," Mrs. V. said. "Tonight I am too tired. Thank you, Jordan. I have not had party for a very long time."

"No, thank you," I said. "Nobody ever threw a party to congratulate me for anything before. It was real nice."

"If only Heinrich had come," she sighed, sitting down on the couch. "He said he would." She seemed distracted, like her mind were someplace else. "I want him to meet you. You are my two boys, yah?"

"Well, he must be very busy, I guess."

"No, I think he is mad at me," she said, looking down at the floor. "You remember that night you help me bury the skull, yah? Well, it was because Heinrich wanted to take it. He wanted to sell it to someone, and I tell him no, but Heinrich is very, what you say, head-strong."

"Oh," I said, feeling a knot suddenly tighten in my stomach.

"And greedy. He is not good boy like you. No, he is not."

CHAPTER ELEVEN

Another Kind of Party

IT WAS A WEEK AFTER MRS. V.'S PARTY that Cullen had his end-of-school blast. His parents had taken off some-place for a week and left the house to Cullen and Geoff. I guess, in a way, we partied every day at the pool after exams, but halfway through the week Geoff announced that there'd be a real party at the house on Saturday night.

"Who's coming?" I asked. And, okay, I admit I was thinking of Kathryn.

"Everybody," he said, shrugging his shoulders. "The word is out."

"Should be good," Nick declared. He sat beside the pool in a baggy bathing suit, his stomach flopping over the waistband. "Besides, we're running out of booze. People should bring enough that there'll be leftovers."

"Yeah, your parents didn't leave much," Mordock chimed in. Lately, he and Nick had become best buddies.

"I haven't noticed you adding to the supply," Cullen said in that way of his. That's what I really admired about him, the way he could put somebody down in this easy, subtle way, and then smile at the victim as if he'd done nothing at all.

Mordock looked embarrassed. "Yeah, well neither does Jordan," he replied.

"So where do I get booze?" I asked. "My mom doesn't drink and all the countess has is schnapps."

"Yah, schnapps is good, yah?" Ryan joked. He sounded more Swedish than German, but the effect still worked. Everybody laughed.

"Besides, Jordan's been initiated," Cullen pointed out. "He brought us the skull. Now what have you done for us, Mordock?"

There was an awkward silence while that truth sank in. Mordock had been hanging out with the guys for a couple of weeks, and somehow his initiation never seemed to happen. Maybe Cullen and Geoff hadn't come up with one yet. Or maybe they were waiting for Mordock to invent something for himself. Still, it was a sore point.

Anyway, getting ready for Cullen's party was a lot different than getting ready for Mrs. V.'s. We didn't bother with any fixing up because everybody knew the house would be a wreck afterwards. There wasn't any caterer or wine glasses or fresh flowers in vases, just another case of beer — which I paid for — and a pile of chips and cheese munchies that looked like it would half-fill Cullen's pool.

There was only one thing we did for decorations, which everybody thought was pretty cool idea at the time. We took the quartz skull from the basement and put it up in a bedroom window overlooking the pool. Then Cullen got one of those old-fashioned Christmas spotlights and set it up behind the skull. When he turned the light on and its filters rotated, the head would glow white, then green, then red, then blue. It was eerie, even in broad daylight. At night, we figured, it would be awesome.

I can't remember what I told my mother so I could get out that night. I think I lied and said something about a sleepover at Cullen's, just in case I collapsed and spent the whole night there.

Cullen had loaned me one of his expensive Hawaiian shirts, and I wore my own bathing suit and sandals. I put a temporary tattoo on my thigh and figured, when I looked at myself in the mirror, that I looked pretty good. The me who had looked like a ten-year-old kid in the spring now looked like a pretty cool teenager. I even decided to shave before the party, just to remove the little bit of hair that grew over my upper lip. Mrs. V.'s husband's razor did a pretty good job, even if it was an antique.

Cullen and the rest of the gang were obviously at the house early, getting into my case of beer before the party even started. Not much else happened until after nine o'clock when the rest of the kids started piling in. Cullen cranked up the stereo and stuck the speakers outside on the deck facing the pool. Ryan acted as the DJ until one of Geoff's friends came in and pushed him off the sound system. It was Geoff and some girls I didn't know who started the dancing. Then a bunch more people came in about ten o'clock, and pretty soon both the pool and the deck were full. The party was noisy and crazy and all, but still good. When I checked, it looked like the glowing skull was smiling at us from its place in the window.

"You look like you're having fun," I heard from over my shoulder.

I turned towards the voice. "Kathryn," I said, "I was hoping you'd come." Was that smooth? Okay, I admit I stole the line from an old movie, but it still came out sounding perfect.

"Yeah, well, I'm here," Kathryn said. "So are we dancing or what?"

Yes, we were dancing! And I ought to tell you that I don't even know how to dance, but that didn't really matter. Kathryn looked so utterly hot in this tube top and wraparound dress that I would have danced with her even if I'd been in a full-body cast. I mean, some offers you don't refuse.

After a few dances, we sat over on the patio to do a little talking. Ryan shot me a look from the distance and then shook his head, but I wasn't paying much attention. I was looking into Kathryn's eyes, just like she'd told me to that first time.

So I was surprised when Mordock came up and plunked himself down right next to us. He definitely wasn't invited.

"So great party, eh?" he said, to nobody in particular.

"Yeah, absolutely," I agreed, then tried to shoot him a get-lost look. He wasn't paying attention. As I learned later on, he wasn't just making conversation.

"So listen, Jordan. I don't want to butt in, but there's something I wanted to ask you."

The music was pounding in my ears so I could barely hear him. "Yeah, what?"

"This old lady you work for ..."

"The countess," I corrected. Then I smiled at Kathryn and she smiled back.

"Yeah, her," Mordock said. "That skull is so cool, we were wondering if she had, like, more stuff. You know, maybe other cool stuff or jewelry or something?"

"Who's asking?"

"Nobody, just wondering," Mordock replied.

"Keep wondering," I snapped at him, annoyed.

Then I turned back to Kathryn. There must have been something about the party, or the moonlight, or the end of exams but I just started blabbing to her about how beautiful she was, and how soft her hair felt on my arm, and how gorgeous her eyes were. I don't know where all the words came from, but they certainly worked a kind of magic. Kathryn sighed and told me how sweet I was, and how much more serious I was than the older guys she knew. Then she kissed me, and I confess I glowed myself at that point — not like the skull in the window, but from inside. I'd never had a girl even like me before, and now I'd had my very first kiss.

For the next few hours we danced and drank and joked and goofed around together. I remember somebody saying something about a midnight swim in the pool, but Kathryn wasn't interested and I don't even know if it actually happened. All I really remember is when Kathryn leaned back against me and I began stroking her hair and, well, it was about as good as you can imagine.

So I didn't notice the people who came in around midnight — a whole crew of guys from the senior high school, and then a bunch from some other school, and then a bunch from nobody knew where. Everybody was pretty blasted by then, and it didn't seem to matter when the first guys were thrown into the pool. But then, somehow, it got out of hand. Some of the new guys tried to throw in some of the girls, and then somebody screamed, and then somebody threw the first punch.

We were all so wired and so drunk and so crazy that maybe anything could have set it off. But the first punch led to others, and more screaming, and then it got really wild. I remember some guy I'd never seen came by and grabbed at Kathryn, just like that, and she pushed him away and I ... I took a swing at him. It was crazy. This guy was way bigger than me, and probably stronger, and drunk out of his mind. But I still took a swing at him. And when I missed the first time, I swung again. This time I connected, and blood started coming down this guy's chin. I think he fell down, but I didn't have time to see him hit the floor because Kathryn dragged me by the arm and pulled me out of there.

It's a good thing, too, because the police cars were already coming down the street, heading for Cullen's house.

CHAPTER TWELVE

Sirens in the Night

I WALKED KATHRYN HOME THAT NIGHT. The air was warm and she was beautiful and I'd been wonderful, she said. So I wasn't surprised when she gave me a deep kiss on the little porch in front of her house. It was warm and wonderful and sexy — everything you might imagine from a kiss like that.

So I was flying pretty high when I walked back to my house. I didn't care much about the party, or the guys or the police breaking everything up. I wasn't thinking about any of that. I was thinking about Kathryn ... and Kathryn ... and Kathryn.

I managed to sneak into my house some time around two. The place was pretty quiet, so I went to get some milk out of the fridge and was surprised to see my sister when I turned around.

"What are you doing up?" I asked her.

"Couldn't sleep," she said, yawning. "I thought you had a sleepover."

"I, uh, it ended kind of early," I said. "You want some milk?"

"Yeah, please," she said as I poured. Miss P. can be surprisingly polite in the middle of the night. "Jordie, what's that red stuff on your hands?"

I looked down and knew right away what she was talking about. It was blood, blood from that guy's chin. "Uh, paint," I lied. Not bad for a quick lie. "We were painting."

"At a sleepover?" she asked.

"Well, it's kind of a guy thing," I told her. Now that seemed pretty laughable, but it took care of Miss P.'s curiosity so we were both able to go upstairs and get some sleep. Apparently she slept right through the night.

I wasn't so lucky.

I didn't hear the police cars when they first arrived, maybe because they didn't have their sirens on. But the flashing red light outside must have woken me up, or else the strange, echoey noise that cops make on their walkie-talkies.

I sat up in bed. Was it us? A fire. Were we on fire, or what?

In a second, I had bolted out of bed and looked outside. There were no fire trucks, only police cars — three of them. And they weren't in front of our house but over at Mrs. von Loewen's.

Oh no, I thought, a heart attack.

I threw on some clothes and raced down the stairs. Neither my mother nor my sister seemed to be up, so I just unlocked the three locks on the door and dashed across the street.

The front door to Mrs. von Loewen's house was open and there were cops standing around, walking over the front lawn and out in back, stepping on the garden I had planted. When I reached the door, I heard a male voice.

"Hey, kid. Where do you think you're going?" It was a cop. He was young and about seven feet tall.

"I, uh, I saw the lights. And … is she okay?"

"How about we start with who you are," the cop said. He took out a notebook and a pencil.

"I'm Jordan. Jordan Bellemare, and I live just over there," I pointed. "I do, uh, yard work for Mrs. von Loewen."

"Yard work?"

"Yeah, like gardening and digging and all that. Listen, is she okay?"

"She's fine," he said. "We've called her son and he's on the way over."

Heinrich, I thought. The son who never shows his face around here and doesn't even come to his mother's garden party. But there was nothing I could say or do.

"What happened?"

"There's been a break-and-enter," he said. His walkie-talkie blared something and he talked into it for a couple of seconds. I looked past him into the house. The place was a mess. Stuff was tossed and thrown all over the place, like it had been searched by the Three Stooges. All the drawers in the dining room buffet were pulled out. Half of the clocks were thrown to the floor. The doors on the little lamps tables were open, and all the junk in there was thrown to the floor.

When the cop put his phone away, I asked the obvious question again. "But she's okay?"

"Shaken up, but okay," the cop said. "Somebody did this when she was asleep upstairs. She woke up but got smart and locked her door."

"She must have been scared out of her mind."

"Probably. But she'll be okay. So how about I get a little more from you," the cop began, and then peppered me with a few dozen questions. I didn't have many answers. Yes, the house had a burglar alarm, but she almost never turned it on. Yes, the windows locked pretty well — I knew that because I cleaned them. The house was always locked up; I made sure of it.

"Any idea who might have done this?" the cop asked. "Did the occupant have any quarrels with anybody? Any kids in the neighborhood who do this kind of thing?"

"She's just a nice old lady, that's all. And I don't think any kids in the neighborhood … I mean, mostly they're little kids."

He looked at me strangely.

"Look, can I at least talk to her? I mean, Mrs. von Loewen counts on me. When there's a problem, I help her out. I do. I really do."

"I've got to wait for the son to come over and we'll ask him. Mrs. von Loon is upstairs talking to the detective right now.

"Von Loewen," I corrected.

"Whatever. The detective will probably want to talk to you too, maybe tomorrow." And then he got my phone number. "Might as well go home and get some sleep, son. Nothing to do here, really. The fingerprint people will want everything left just like this until they're done."

I nodded, dumbly. I didn't know what else to say. The "adults" had taken over and weren't going to listen to me.

"Somebody will call you," the cop said, looking at me as if he wondered why I hadn't already disappeared.

"Yeah," I said, and turned to go. Inside the house, I could hear something. It was faint at first, an indistinct sound muffled by the walls. But the closer I listened, the more I knew what it was. Mrs. von Loewen was upstairs somewhere, sobbing.

I spent that long, sleepless night with the police lights flashing through the blinds into my room and the burble of their radios crackling through my brain. I felt dazed and clueless.

A house invasion, that's what they call it, like a robbery could be some kind of military maneuver. Some gang had busted into Mrs. von Loewen's house and torn it apart while the countess had to hide upstairs. She was probably afraid for her life, not sure if they were going to burst through the bedroom door and kill her, too.

I kept seeing the whole thing in my mind — the house-wrecking, the sheer terror that Mrs. von Loewen had to feel. I mean, she didn't even have a phone in her room. She told me once that it was impolite to talk to people on the phone from the bedroom so she didn't have a phone anywhere on the second floor.

My brain kept running everything over again. If only I'd been there, or been awake, or been listening ... well, maybe I could have been the hero I always wanted to be. Or if I'd checked the basement windows ... maybe it would never have happened at all.

Later, half asleep, I replayed the scene in different ways, with different heroic rescues or smart maneuvers. I made myself a James Bond or a Mission Impossible guy, doing just the right thing to stop the house invasion. And at least once that night I woke up from a nightmare — the skull, the quartz skull, was laughing at me.

So you can imagine how awful I felt the next morning. Fortunately, my mom had gone shopping some place so I didn't have to talk to her. Miss P. must have slept through the whole thing, because she didn't say anything to me while munching her Cheerios.

When I looked across the street, there was a very plain Chevy parked in front of Mrs. von Loewen's house. It was the kind of vehicle that flashed "unmarked police car" to anyone who looked at it. There was also a nice Audi that I'd never seen before — maybe Heinrich's car.

I figured it was time to get over there and see what I could do. I mean, somebody had to clean up the mess, and there was no way the countess would be able to do it. So I threw on some clothes and splashed some water on my face. Then I ran across the rain-soaked street and knocked on the door.

My knock was answered by a gray-haired man who walked in the same straight-up fashion as Mrs. von Loewen. With him was a burly guy in a brown suit.

"Hi, I'm … uh, Jordan. I do the yard work for Mrs. von Loewen."

The burly guy eyeballed me. I could almost tell he was a cop by the car, the suit and the way he seemed to memorize my face. The gray-haired guy said nothing.

"I was just wondering how she is," I mumbled. "Mrs. von Loewen, that is. I thought maybe I could help clean up."

"You know something about the robbery?" the detective asked, suddenly very interested in me.

"Well, I know there was a break-in. I live right there," I pointed to my bedroom window, "so it's not like I could sleep through it." My words came out kind of snarky, but I was too tired to care. "Listen, I really just want to know she's okay."

"She's probably fine," the gray-haired man said. "I took her to the hospital for observation. A lot of stress, some heart arrhythmia."

I nodded, though I didn't have any idea what "arrhythmia" meant.

"So you're Heinrich," I said.

"And you must be Jordan," he replied, smiling just a little. "My mother talks about you a great deal. You did a fine job on the gazebo."

"Uh, thanks," I said, wondering why he had brought that up. "But is she really okay? I mean, what is arrhythmia?"

"It just means that her heart is beating a little bit irregularly," Heinrich explained. "The doctors say it should fix itself in a day or so. She'll be fine."

The cop butted into our talk. "Son, you know anything about the basement window being unlocked?"

"Is that how they got in?"

"Looks like it," he said. "You ever go down to the basement when you worked around the house?"

"Sure, that's where the tools are," I said. And then I figured out where all this was going, and that made me mad. "But I didn't leave any windows unlocked," I snapped. "I lock up the house even when Mrs. V. forgets."

"I'm not suggesting," the cop said, backing off. "Just asking."

"Detective Bartkowski," Heinrich said, "I think you should leave Jordan alone and try to round up some real suspects. Somebody out there has my mother's pearls and a life-sized quartz skull."

My heart stopped. I was ready to say something about the skull, about it being buried and all, but of course it wasn't buried ... and I really didn't know where it was any more. Something about the way the cop looked at me told me to play dumb. "They ... they stole her pearls?"

"Yes, pearls, jewelry, money — my mother kept them all in that Chinese cabinet in the living room," Heinrich told me. "She's very upset about the pearls, as you can imagine."

"She brought them ... brought them with her from the old country," I said, though he must have known. "They were all she had from back then."

"Well, my mother is a bit melodramatic," Heinrich said, "but she loved her pearls and some were very precious. Frankly, I'm more concerned about the quartz skull. I had just made an arrangement with a collector who was willing to pay a fair amount of money for it. And now that's gone too."

"Mrs. von Loewen said, well, she said that there was a curse," I mumbled.

"My mother and her stories," he said, shaking his head. "The curse is entirely in her imagination, like much of the rest of what she tells people. But the skull is real and it's gone. She kept it quite well hidden, even from me, so somebody had to know it was in the house to find it."

"Uh, maybe your mom hid it someplace else," I said, though I knew so much more. I felt like I had guilt written all over my face.

"That would be just like her," Heinrich sighed.

"Listen, son," the cop broke in. "Keep your ears open, okay? You might just hear something that would help us on this one. Maybe some kids who start bragging about it, or showing off this quartz skull. You never know. Give me a call if you find out anything," he added, handing me a business card.

"Yeah, yeah, I will," I said. My brain was turning around like crazy. Something was there — an idea was almost there.

I trudged off to my house while the two men watched me go. They were still talking, maybe about me for all I knew, but my brain was trying to work something through. If I wasn't so desperate for sleep maybe I could think straight, maybe I could finish the idea that was trying to form in my head.

When I got to my house, I didn't even make it up

to the bedroom. I fell asleep on the couch. When I woke up thirty minutes later, I sat bolt upright. I had only one thought it my mind, and it was crystal clear.

Mordock did it.

CHAPTER THIRTEEN

The Pearls

I WASN'T IN MY RIGHT MIND WHEN I STORMED OUT of the house. I was mad. I was so crazy mad that I didn't have a plan or a strategy or even a half-formed idea of what I was going to do. All I knew was that Mordock had done the break-in, maybe with Cullen and the rest of the gang, or maybe just a couple of them. But it was them. It was Mordock's initiation — break in, steal something, and terrorize an old lady. The more I thought about that, the more I felt a burning in my gut and in my brain, a strange fireball inside me of anger and outrage.

All I knew for sure is that I was going to get back the pearls that Mrs. von Loewen had saved when she fled the old country. That was the simple part of it. Maybe I couldn't get back her money, but I'd hammer Mordock and get the pearls and take them back to her. That much I could do. That was the *least* I could do.

I scribbled some lame excuse to my mother, then took off for Cullen's house. I kind of half-walked and half-ran the entire distance. All the time, I kept trying to get my brain to work right. What was I going to do when I got there? Storm in and confront them all? Nah. That would be crazy — and I was crazy, all right, but not *that* crazy. I'd have to be smarter. I'd have to out-smart them just like they outsmarted me. A hero has got to be smart, right?

By the time I reached Cullen's house, I was soaked from the drizzle. The house and its lawn looked like a tornado had come through. There were bottles and glasses thrown all over, even some now-soggy toilet paper strewn through the bushes. I hadn't seen any of that the night before, but I hadn't been paying much attention. I'd spent the whole evening blinded by Kathryn and the party and the guys. I'd been a fool.

I went up to the front door and got ready to pound on it. But I stopped. What was I going to say? You did it — you took it — give me the pearls! Yeah, right. I did-n't even know which of them had been in on it. I was pretty certain it was Mordock's idea, so Nick would have been part of it. But what about Cullen and Geoff and Ryan? Maybe they didn't know anything. And what proof did I have, anyhow? Sure, all the pieces fit togeth-er, but so what? Circumstantial evidence, that's all. I stood there and actually remembered the phrase, *cir-cumstantial evidence*. Useless. I needed some serious proof. I needed to find the pearls, or something.

So I ducked over to the east side, where the pool security fence had a locked gate. Somebody had broken that last night, so it was easy to get in. When I peered around the corner, I saw that the whole backyard had been trashed. Food, broken glass, smashed patio furniture, a speaker floating in the swimming pool. The end of the party must have been a real disaster, but now everything was quiet.

I looked up at the central bedroom window, but the skull was no longer there. I could only hope that somehow it was still in the house.

I darted along the back and tried the patio door. Locked. To one side was a basement window. It was half open already. I took my house key and sliced the screen, then pushed the screen up and slid out the half window. Easy as pie. Probably the same way they had broken into Mrs. von Loewen's house.

I waited for Cullen's house alarm to go off, but nothing happened. Chances are that the alarm was smashed up last night, too. So I slid out the other half window and that gave me enough room to drop down inside. I landed in a storage room that was full of boxes, old bikes, pool supplies; but no sign of the stolen pearls. In fact, there was enough dust that I figured nothing had moved around here for quite a while.

I went over to the door and moved silently out to the basement hallway that led to the family room with the big TV. The guys and I had spent plenty of time watching DVDs down there. So I went with my hunch ... quiet ... quiet. The house was almost too quiet.

I peeked through the door to the family room and saw no one. The room was trashed, but not that much worse than usual. The only thing that seemed out of place was a small garbage bag in one corner. I mean, nothing else had been cleaned up on the lawn, or at the pool, or in this room. But there was this garbage bag, just sitting there.

I felt so pumped. My hands were trembling as I grabbed the bag and reached inside. And there they were, strand after strand of pearls. Mrs. von Loewen's pearls. They'd be worth thousands, maybe more, if Mordock could find anybody to take them, but they were worth far more to the countess. I had to get them back to her. Then I'd come back, find the skull and deal with Mordock and the rest of them.

I began moving toward the family room door … quiet, quiet. I'd be out of there in no time. I'd be clear …

Except there was somebody on the other side of the door, somebody big.

"What took you so long, kid?"

It was Nick. Right behind him were Mordock, Cullen and Geoff. Only Ryan was missing.

"Took you long enough to get back here," Mordock chimed in.

"He was too busy making out with Ryan's sister," Cullen pointed out. "And we were all a little busy last night," he added. His voice was so cold that I wanted to strangle him.

"So what do you think of my initiation, eh?" Mordock asked. He was bragging, as if stealing from an old lady were somehow cool or courageous.

I clutched the pearls to my chest and stared at the three of them. My brain was calculating odds — getting past them to the door, zero; outrunning them, zero; beating them up, minus zero. And then something turned over in my head. The terrified little kid in me faded away and somebody new, maybe a man, a real man, came to the surface. Suddenly there was a transformation — I wasn't scared any more. I decided to tell them exactly what I thought.

"I think it stinks," I began. My body was trembling and the words were a little shaky, but the man inside me didn't stop. "I thinks it was stupid and mean. I think only a miserable coward would break into an old lady's house and steal the stuff she loves. You guys are …" I looked at all of them, and then let go with more swear words than I even knew were in me.

I don't know how long my swearing would have continued, but Nick stopped it when he came over and delivered a sucker punch right to my gut.

The pain shot through me, sizzling and white. I lost my grip on the pearls as his punch hit me, making it easy for Geoff to take the garbage bag from my arms. When Nick landed his second punch, to my face, I fell to the floor. I felt like I was going to throw up.

"All right, leave him alone," Cullen ordered.

Nick backed off. Mordock picked up the bag of pearls and cradled it like a baby. Geoff threw me on the couch. The pain in my stomach felt hot, like some glowing coal in my gut. My face, too, was on fire.

"Mordock's initiation was," Cullen paused to come up with a word, "unfortunate. There was some bad luck, really."

"We didn't think the old lady would wake up," Mordock explained.

I croaked out my amazement. "You thought she'd sleep through you trashing the place?"

"Look, we were drunk," he said.

"Hey, you don't have to apologize to this guy," Nick barked, looking at the others. "It was a cool idea, and we can use the money. All of us."

"But not the jewelry, Nick," Geoff broke in. Sometimes he did this, acting like the voice of authority because he was three years older than the rest of us and he could treat everyone else like a kid. "That's grand theft. You have any idea what these pearls are worth? We could all be sent up for years."

"So the pearls go back," Cullen said decisively. "Jordan can take them back and figure out some way to cover. He knows how to keep his mouth shut."

"Why should I?" I shot back.

"Let's start with you telling us about the old lady's stuff," Mordock said.

"I didn't," I whined. But even as I said it, I knew that I *had* told them all about Mrs. von Loewen's wealth. I had bragged about it to Mordock and Kathryn just last night. It was all stupid, but true.

"Of course, you did bring us the skull," Geoff added.

"And then we can say you left open the basement window," Mordock said slyly.

"So, from anyone's perspective, Jordan, you're in on this," Cullen said to sum it up. "You're implicated."

"I'd say that Jordan was the brains behind the whole thing, don't you think?" Nick added with a sick smile on his face.

"So if we go down, you go down," Cullen declared.

I sat there, dripping sweat, pain radiating from my gut, feeling like a knife were being twisted into my soul. The others seemed cool, almost enjoying all this.

"Our best advice," Geoff concluded, "is that you take the pearls back and keep your mouth shut about all this."

"And the skull?" I said.

"Well, we do have to apologize about that," Cullen went on as if he were a corporate lawyer. "We're afraid that the skull isn't here right now. Someone seems to have borrowed it during the party. But when it turns up, you can cheerfully give it back to the old lady."

"Unless you rat out. You don't even want to think about what happens if you rat," Nick said, screwing up his face as if he were looking at some sad hospital case.

Nick grabbed me by one arm and started pulling me up the stairs. I resisted only a little. There wasn't any point to fighting back, not against these odds. He tossed me out the front door and Geoff threw my baseball cap so it landed at my feet. Then Mordock tossed the bag of pearls at me.

"You're smart, Jordan, so figure out a good story and give the old lady her pearls back. Just be a good kid, and it will all turn out fine." Cullen told me. Nick snorted at this advice and Geoff shook his head. They slammed the door and left me sitting on the front steps.

After a minute or two, I got up and staggered to the driveway. I wanted to stand up. I didn't want them laughing at me from inside the house. I wanted to walk away like a man, or at least like a human being.

So I did. I pulled myself up, took the bag of pearls in my arms, and began walking carefully, one step, two steps, down the sidewalk toward my house. By the time I reached the end of the street, no one would have suspected what had just happened to me, or the fix I was in. But I knew. I couldn't get the whole miserable thing out of my head — my stupidity, my foolishness.

When I knew I was far enough from the house that they couldn't see me, I stopped and sat down on the curb. I put my head in my hands and started throwing up. Everything. Everything.

CHAPTER FOURTEEN

A Choice

WHEN I GOT HOME, I DITCHED THE BAG OF PEARLS in the garage, right where I'd hidden the skull weeks before. Our car was gone so I knew my mother had gone out someplace. That was the good news. I didn't want her to see me as I was — beaten up in more ways than one. The bad news is that my sister greeted me at the door. "Jordan, you look sick," she said. There was more curiosity in her voice than concern.

"Yeah, I am."

"Mom's at a meeting and she told me to tell you something." Her voice trailed off. I think the message had already dissolved in her memory.

"Like what?"

"Somebody called. The son of the old lady, Mrs. von Loon ... that one. Anyway, he called and said she wanted to see you, or maybe he wanted to see you. Something like that."

I was ready to shake her. Miss P. can be such an idiot! "Which one? At home? At the hospital? Where?"

"I dunno. I mean, I can't remember. No, now I do. Valley General, like the hospital, I think."

Eight years old, I said to myself. What can you expect?

"Jordan, you in some kind of trouble?"

"No, no trouble," I lied. "I'm fine. Really."

"You're acting kind of weird is all. And your shoes stink. It smells like you threw up on them," she concluded, and then went skipping off to the television set.

I pulled off the lousy running shoes and threw them in the garbage. Then I went to my room and lay down on the bed. I wanted to be eight again. I wanted to have a simple life and simple friends someplace, anyplace but here. I wanted not to mess up and hurt people. I wanted to do things right.

And after a few minutes, I had a pretty good sense of what I had to do. I scribbled a quick note to my mom, then went down to the corner to grab a bus to the hospital. The afternoon rain had lifted and now the sky was filled with fluffy white clouds.

When finally I got to the hospital, the receptionist gave me a funny look. I saw my own reflection in the elevator and realized that I still had some dried blood on my chin. I guess I looked more like a patient than a visitor. Somebody who should be going to emergency after a fight, not the nice neighbor kid going to visit a sweet old lady.

Still, I got the ward location and made my way up to the fifth floor, cleaning up my face along the way. The hospital halls and elevator had that medicinal disinfectant smell, kind of a boozy Lysol aroma that was so strong it hid my own stink.

I got to the ward area and checked with the nurse, who couldn't find Mrs. von Loewen's name. She wasn't under the v's, just Mrs. Hildegard Loewen. I guess when you're a patient, things like the "von" get lost. Anyway, the nurse finally told me the room number and then said I had only about twenty minutes until they'd kick me out.

I left the nursing station and went down the hall to 5-012, a room with two beds and thin cloth dividers separating one from another. Mrs. von Loewen had a bed by the window; her son was sitting on a chair, reading a book when I came to the door.

"Oh, uh, John," he said, looking up at me.

"Jordan," I corrected him. "Is she … asleep?"

"No," Mrs. von Loewen said in a low voice, "I rest my eyes, Jordan. I knew you would come. You are such good boy."

Why did that hurt so much? Why did those words make my heart contract in my chest?

"How do you feel?" I asked her. She looked pale, but not very different from the way she usually was around her house.

"Good, good," she said. "Heinrich, you fix pillows."

Her son put aside his book and propped her head up with the pillows. Then he asked his mother if she wanted some water. Her answer was a no, in German, and so he sat back down.

"Jordan, I need you to look after the garden, yah? The flowers, they need water. And weeds, you pull out weeds for me, okay?"

"Sure," I said, "no problem."

"My son does not want me to go home right away. He is very headstrong boy, my Heinrich."

"Mo-om," her son said. It was the same whine that I used in talking to my mother, except that Heinrich was fifty or more.

"But I am a headstrong woman, so we see who wins. We don't let thugs chase us out of house, no, is not like the old country back then. *Vincerò*, Jordan. You know what that means?"

"Uh, no."

"We will win," she said — *ve vill vin*, it came out. "We will triumph."

"Mom, you've tried living on your own," her son piped up, "and this just shows you it doesn't work. You're too, too — I don't know — vulnerable."

"Oh, I wish you were more like your father!" she snapped back. "He knew what courage was. He knew not to be afraid. And I am not afraid or, how you say, vulnerable. I don't even know this word, vulnerable. What I know is, I don't need to be here. I want to go home, to my *heimat*. Jordan, you tell him I just want to go home."

I looked at the two of them and didn't know really what to say. It was like getting into the middle of a family argument. "I, uh, think you said it yourself, Mrs. V. If you're feeling okay, well, you should go home."

Heinrich shot me an angry look, then turned to his mother. "One more day, Mom. As soon as your heartbeat stabilizes, that's all. You've had a shock and you have to be careful."

"Yah, yah, yah, careful ... always careful," she said with scorn. "Jordan, you push button so I can sit up more, okay?"

There were actually about three buttons at the foot of the bed, but her son hit the right one before I had to start figuring them out. With a grinding of gears, the top of the bed started moving up until Mrs. von Loewen was about half-vertical.

"Now Jordan, did you hear, my pearls they stole?" she looked hurt.

"And the quartz skull, and money, and who knows what else," Heinrich added.

"Yes, yes, but only the pearls matter. The skull, I told you, we buried the skull. And money, what is money? But memories, Heinrich, the pearls are my memories."

Heinrich seemed unimpressed, but I knew what she meant. I knew how important the pearls were.

"The police, they have fingerprints from the window," Heinrich said. "but no matches yet. It wasn't anybody with a record, just kids."

"Big kids," Mrs. von Loewen said, "I could hear them. They were big, like you, Jordan."

I turned red. I could feel the heat on my face, but nobody else seemed to notice.

"I was so afraid when I heard them, but there was no phone, so all I could do was lock the door."

"I'm getting you another phone, mom."

"Yah, yah, after the cow runs away the barn door gets fixed, always. Next time, I keep a baseball bat by the bed."

"Well, I'm not sure that's a good idea," I piped up. I could just picture Mrs. von Loewen, all hundred pounds of her, trying to take on Nick with a baseball bat. Then again, why should she have to worry about the Nicks and Mordocks out there? Why should an old lady have to barricade herself inside her bedroom while her entire house gets turned upside down?

Mrs. von Loewen's son was just shaking his head. I guess he thought his mother was a little batty, but he didn't say anything directly. "You haven't heard anything about the robbery, have you, Jordan?" he asked me.

It was an idle question. I could have said no and gone on to talk about the weather, or Mrs. V.'s health, or the garden, or anything. I could have done what

Cullen demanded, kept my mouth shut and covered for all of them, and for me. After all, I was the one who looked the most guilty. I was the one who had access to the house, and knew about the pearls, and even had them sitting in my garage.

On my way to the hospital, I had even come up with a plan to explain my recovery of the pearls — an anonymous phone tip, somebody called me after I let the word out that I wanted the pearls back. I mean, it was a lie, but I'd look good and Mrs. V. would be happy enough.

But I knew, right then, that I couldn't live with a lie like that. It wasn't a matter of whether or not I could *get away* with a lie; it had to do with what kind of person I wanted to be. Right now, I was just a lonely, scared kid — that much was true. But once I had wanted to be a superhero, I had wanted so much to defend truth, justice and all that. Those things still mattered, regardless of all the cynical stuff you hear. I don't think old ladies should have to be scared or robbed by kids doing a break-in on a dare. I don't think I want to be part of a gang that terrorizes people for fun, or steals things for a joke. I think, just like Mrs. V. thinks, that the world should be better than that.

And I'm better than that.

Decided to tell the truth. It was, I think, the gutsiest thing I ever did. I looked into the tired eyes of Mrs. V.'s son and said, "I know who did it."

"What?" Heinrich asked, suddenly paying me serious attention.

"You do?" Mrs. von Loewen echoed.

I could feel the blood rushing to my head. I was sweating already, and I hadn't really said anything yet. I turned to the countess. "Yeah, I know. I went over to their house to make sure and … and I saw the pearls. And I, uh, I got the pearls back for you."

"Oh, wonderful, wonderful," Mrs. von Loewen cried. "Jordan, you are wonderful. You are a hero, for sure, a hero."

But Heinrich was suspicious. He was looking hard at me. "You just walked over and confronted these kids?"

"No, I kind of snuck in," I admitted. "I had a hunch who had done the break-in, but I wanted to be sure. So I got into the house and found the pearls. But then they found me."

"Who?" he said. "You know who they were?"

"Cullen Thurston, his brother Geoff, another kid named Nick and a guy named Mordock."

"So did you tell the police?" he asked.

"No, n-not yet," I stammered. "There's a problem, see. If I tell anybody, they're going to blame me for everything. They're going to say that I left the window unlocked and set the whole thing up."

"Oh, Jordan, that is so stupid. No one would believe that," Mrs. von Loewen said. "No one!"

She was wrong on the last part. I could tell by the way Heinrich was looking at me that he suspected I was part of it. I could see the anger in his eyes. But there was nothing else I could do but go ahead with the truth. The truth shall set you free, somebody said. But the more I talked, the more I feared the truth would get me in trouble.

"So *did* you have any part in it?" her son asked. "Did you?"

"I didn't mean to," I began. "It's just that I didn't think. I was kind of bragging about Mrs. von Loewen and how rich she is ..."

"My mother is not rich," Heinrich butted in while I went ahead.

"So maybe that gave them the idea. But that's all. I didn't leave the window open. I didn't know what Mordock was planning. I didn't ... I never wanted ...." And then I started crying. It was pretty pathetic, an almost-grown guy sitting there, crying like a child. I certainly wasn't a superhero at that moment, not even an ordinary, run-of-the-mill hero. I was just a scared kid.

"Jordan, is okay. I know you didn't. You are good boy," she said, trying to soothe me.

Her son didn't seem quite so sure. "So are you ready to tell all this to the police? Will you do that?"

"Yeah, I'm ready," I said, wiping away the tears. "I just had to tell Mrs. V. first. So you'd know, before all the lies started."

"Jordan, Jordan. It will be all right," she said, patting my sticky hair with her hand. "You do what is right and you can never regret it. That is what I always tell Heinrich. *Richt is immer richt.*"

"Sure, Mom," he said. Then he turned to me, "Jordan, I think we should go make a phone call. You've got some tough questions to answer."

"Yeah, I know," I told him. But now I was ready.

CHAPTER FIFTEEN

Fallout

I MADE THE PHONE CALL and didn't get Detective Bartkowski. The switchboard gave me some other cop who took down the information I gave him over the phone without much comment. He asked me to come down to the station and do it all again, officially, so I said okay and hung up. I didn't feel heroic or righteous or anything like that. Mostly I felt rotten. Add to that the suspicious looks I kept getting from Heinrich, and I started to get angry.

After all, I could have kept my mouth shut. There was no bonus for me in telling what I knew or going to the cops or admitting anything. If I'd kept the secret, there was a chance that Cullen and his gang would still let me hang out with them. I might even get a cool reputation around school, or maybe have been able to keep seeing Kathryn.

But I told the truth. I had to. I wanted to keep working for the countess without having to feel guilty, every day, for my part in the break-in. I wanted to live the rest of my life knowing I hadn't backed down to

Nick, or been too afraid to stand up for people who mattered to me. And I wanted to look at my face in the morning and not be disgusted at the guy looking back.

But then came the fallout.

Fallout. It's an old word that comes from the days of nuclear bombs. Apparently if you survive the initial atomic blast, then little radioactive particles will rain down on you hours and days later and still kill you quite nicely. So far, I had survived the blast: a punch to the stomach, a threat, the embarrassment of the truth itself. But the fallout would come down on me for months after.

The police did a search right after I made my official statement and ended up charging Nick and Mordock. By then, the money had disappeared, but Mordock's fingerprints were all over the window and Nick's matched some in the house. Apparently Cullen, Geoff and Ryan said they knew nothing and weren't part of it. Maybe they weren't; I'll never know for sure.

From what I heard when school started again, the gang fell apart after the party and the robbery. Cullen and Geoff were seriously grounded by their parents, but more because of the party than because of the break-in. When I saw Geoff once outside our new senior high school, he was waiting for the bus. I guess his parents had taken away his wheels. Nick and Mordock had a trial that fall and were given some community service time. I knew that because Mrs. V. had to do a victim-impact statement and then go testify. I'm certain that this very elderly old lady, in pearls, must have made quite an impression.

Despite all the threats, nobody ever came after me. Nick never followed through with the beating he had promised, nor did any of the others try to bug me too much at school. Still, they got the word out. I was the guy who couldn't be trusted, who got Nick and Mordock in trouble with the cops, who ratted out his friends. The response at school was immediate: I was either treated like a slimeball or ignored. If I'd been a social zero when I first moved here, my status was way into the negative numbers now.

Word of all this even reached my clueless little sister when she went back to her elementary school. "Jordan, all the kids say that you ratted out your friends." She had this accusing look on her face.

"No. I just figured out what kind of people my friends were," I told her.

"Jaz says she doesn't want to play with me because I'm your sister."

"Tell her that you're only my half-sister. That's the truth, after all."

Miss P. smiled. "I know what's even better. I'll say I'm adopted. I'll tell her that my real parents were, uh, a prince and princess in, uh ...."

"Transylvania," I said with a smirk on my face.

"Yeah, that's good. Transylvania. I like that."

It was only later, after she talked to my mom, that Miss P. changed her mind. She did her little tap-tap-tap on my bedroom door and then stuck her face in.

"Jordie?"

"Yeah."

"I'm sorry about what I said before. About not being your sister."

"Hey, nothing wrong with wanting to be the Princess of Transylvania," I told her.

"But Mom explained everything so I kind of understand it now," she said, looking a bit embarrassed. "So I phoned Jaz and told her I was proud of you."

I didn't ask what Jaz had said back. No sense interfering with Miss P.'s chance to act heroic. She might as well learn early on that there are consequences. Flags don't fly and brass bands don't play. Mostly you just get on with some kind of life.

Even though Ryan wasn't really part of the robbery or what happened after, we were both a little awkward when I saw him at school. We had both been involved, once, and we would always know it. So when we talked, there were these strange blanks in the conversation when it would bump up against stuff that neither of us wanted to remember. Needless to say, my one-night romance with Kathryn went nowhere. Apparently she woke up in the morning to realize that she'd actually kissed a kid in grade nine, and almost puked in her slippers.

Ironically, my one remaining friend in tenth grade turned out to be Jessica, the brainer. She actually had a story published that fall in an SF magazine. One day she said she'd let me see it if I'd buy her a Coke at Ugly George's – as long as I didn't blow smoke in her face. I told her I'd quit the habit, and that led to the first smile I'd seen from her in a long time. And I have to admit, Jessica has a really nice smile.

I read the story later and saw that there was this character named Jordan who was not, as she'd threatened, a pathetic minor figure who gets knocked off in the first couple of pages. I was actually a heroic central character who outsmarts the villains on Centuri 782 and manages to save the main code of the Alpharian Empire. I died later in the story, but at least I had a few splendid paragraphs.

There was one piece of all this that I didn't manage to finish up until school started again and Mrs. V. was back home. Now that she was healthy enough to hear it, I had to tell her about the skull.

"This is serious," I said. "I should have told you before but, well, it's the last piece, really."

"So no schnapps, yah?" she said. "Serious."

"It's about the skull, you know, the skull we buried."

"Yah, and the curse. I blame the skull for what

happened," Mrs. V. said, "to you and to me, both. Heinrich should thank me I never gave to him."

"Well," I hemmed and hawed, "I guess that's part of it. Mrs. V., you *can't* give it to him … I mean, the skull is gone."

"No, is buried."

I shook my head. "That's what I'm trying to explain. Back when I was trying to impress the gang, I dug up the skull—"

"Jordie, no!" she exclaimed.

"Yes, now let me finish," I said. The words and my skin were both burning. "It was stupid, I know, but I dug up the skull and took it to Cullen's house. I was going to leave it there for a couple of weeks and then bury it again, but the skull disappeared during a party and … it's gone. Just gone."

"Ach, that is terrible, terrible."

"I know. I feel terrible."

"No, you should feel bad," Mrs. V. told me, "but not terrible. Was a mistake. If that is your biggest mistake ever, you will have nice life. But some was my fault too. I should have smashed the skull back then. We have axe, we could just smash it to pieces — would have been better. Yah, better. Now the curse goes on."

"I'm sorry."

"So am I," she said. "The skull is gone, but we were all stupid to let it survive."

So we left it at that, at stupidity. But stupidity can be dangerous, as I found out, and maybe the curse wasn't as silly as I thought. The other day I saw a quartz skull for sale on eBay that was a lot like the one that disappeared. There was a bid of twelve thousand dollars on it, so I can see why Heinrich would have wanted to sell the thing. Of course, the one for sale wasn't the skull Mrs. von Loewen's father found. For one thing, it didn't have that really evil smile and it probably didn't have a curse.

I telling you this not because Mrs. V. ever wants it back, or because it's worth a lot of money, but because the skull is out there, somewhere. It might make you greedy, or foolish, or even lose your judgement for a while. That's why you have to be careful.

So I've learned.

About the Author

The author of *The Countess and Me* is Paul Kropp. He's an experienced creator of young-adult fiction whose first work, *Wilted*, was published back in 1978. Since then, he has written fiction for teenagers and younger readers, as well as non-fiction titles for adults.

Paul Kropp's work for young people includes six award-winning young-adult novels, 30 novels for reluctant readers and three humorous books for younger children.

Mr. Kropp's earlier novels for young adults, including *Moonkid and Prometheus*, *Ellen/Elena/Luna* and *Moonkid and Liberty*, have been translated into German, Danish, French, Portuguese and two dialects of Spanish. They have won awards both in Canada and abroad.

Mr Kropp was born in Buffalo, New York in 1948. He took his Bachelor's degree at Columbia, in New York City, and a Master's degree – with a thesis on 17th-century English poetry – at the University of Western Ontario in London. Today, he lives in Toronto, Ontario in a century-old townhouse in the city's Cabbagetown district. He has three sons (Alex, Justin and Jason) and two step-children (Emma and Ken), ages 21 to 34. He taught high-school English in Hamilton, Burlington and Toronto for twenty years, but now spends his time writing and editing.

For more information on Paul Kropp, see the Website: www.paulkropp.com